Books by Matt Christopher

The Year Mom Won the Pennant

The Year Mom

Won the Pennant

Matt Christopher

Illustrations by
Foster Caddell

Little, Brown and Company

BOSTON   TORONTO   LONDON

Republished in 1986

The Library of Congress has cataloged this work as follows:
Christopher, Matt.
    The year Mom won the pennant, [by] Matt Christopher. Illus. by Foster Caddell. [1st ed.] Boston, Little, Brown [1968]
    147 p. illus. 20 cm.
    Summary: The boys are all hesitant when one boy's mother is the only parent who volunteers to coach their Little League team, but there is quite a surprise in store for them.
    [1. Baseball—Fiction] I. Caddell, Foster, illus. II. Title.
PZ7.C458 Ye   [Fic]   68-11110
                               MARC

ISBN 0-316-13954-8   AC
ISBN 0-316-13988-2 (pbk)

                    HC: 10 9
                    PB: 15 14 13

                        VB

          Published simultaneously in Canada
        by Little, Brown & Company (Canada) Limited
          Printed in the United States of America

To
Charlie Foote

The Year Mom Won the Pennant

1

NICK VASSEY drilled the ball straight over the plate. *Boom!* The ball connected solidly with Gale Matson's bat and rocketed over the fence, far left of the foul line.

"Quit pulling that ball!" yelled Cyclone Maylor at second base.

"I'm not pulling it!" Gale yelled back, his face glistening in the hot sun. "I'm hitting it!"

Nick grinned. In spite of the monkey business going on, Gale could make the most sour-looking puss break into a smile.

3

A moment later the smile disappeared. "Isn't anybody going after that ball?" Nick asked.

No one budged. The outfielders and the infielders were standing like statues, some of them with their arms crossed, some even with their ankles crossed.

Pat Krupa, standing near third base, was closest to the ball.

"Go after it, will you, Pat?" pleaded Nick. "We don't have many balls."

Pat glanced at the others behind him, made a face, and went on a slow run after the ball. He had to go out the gate, then swing right behind the fence. "Straighten 'em out next time," he grumbled as he ran by.

This is the trouble when you don't have a coach, thought Nick. No one wants to do anything extra.

Jerry Wong, who was catching the balls

thrown in from the fielders, tossed him a ball. Nick stretched and aimed a pitch at the outside corner. Gale swung and drove the ball inches past Nick's right ear.

"Hey! What have I done to you? Okay, lay this one down, Gale."

Gale bunted the next pitch down the third-base line and beelined for first. Jim Rennie batted next. Finally they all had taken their turns. But Wayne Snow wanted to bat again.

"If you do, everybody else will want to," said Nick. "And we've got to have outfield and infield practice."

"We can have outfield and infield practice the next time," argued Wayne. "Come on, somebody. Pitch to me."

"I'll pitch a couple to you if you'll pitch a couple to me," offered Tom Warren, the team's best hitter last year.

"You're on," said Wayne.

5

"Who's going to shag them?" snapped Scotty Page. "*I'm* not."

Nick looked from one to the other and began to feel wretched. You can't have a team with each guy wanting his own way. It would fall apart in no time.

"You know what's going to happen?" Gale Matson piped up. "There won't be a Thunderballs team, that's what. Not unless we get a coach."

"But Nick says his father doesn't want to coach us any more," Jim Rennie said.

"Why not?" Cyclone turned a surprised look at Nick.

Nick shrugged. "He's working later hours now, so he doesn't have time. And he's never won the pennant. He figures maybe someone else could do better. How about your father, Gale? Have you asked him?"

"He's a cop," Gale answered. "He works different shifts. He can't."

"My dad can't either," said Cyclone. "He's a pilot. He's away a lot."

"How about your dad, Wayne?" Nick asked. "Think he'd like to coach us?"

Wayne shook his head and ran his hand up the full length of his bat. "He doesn't have time either."

"Looks as if the Thunderballs have just fallen apart," announced Russell Gray. "I'm going to get on another team before it's too late."

"It *is* too late," said Nick. "The other teams have been formed."

"Then what are we going to do?"

"I don't know," said Nick.

"You sure, Dad?" Nick pleaded again while Mom and the girls, Jen and Sue, were placing the food on the table. "Are you sure you won't have time to coach this year?"

"I'm sure," replied Dad. "I've told you my reasons, Nick. I'm working more hours. And I've coached the team for four years and have never come close to first place. Give some other father a chance. Maybe he can do better."

"But no other father *wants* to coach us, Dad," exclaimed Nick. "They all have excuses, too. And without a coach, we won't have a team!"

Jen and Sue sat down at their regular places across from Nick, and Mom was across from Dad. After Dad said grace, they began eating. Hamburg, mashed potatoes and corn usually would make Nick forget everything else for a while. But this time the fate of the Thunderballs was uppermost in his mind. What would he do all summer if he didn't play baseball?

"Guess there just won't be any Thunderballs this year," Jen said, putting a forkful of potatoes into her mouth. Her voice, thought Nick, sounded like the knell of doom.

"I have a thought," Mom said.

Nick's ears perked up. "What, Mom? That I play on another team? I can't. It's too late."

"No. Not that."

"What, then, Mom?"

Mom's eyes twinkled. "Okay if I tried it? Coaching the Thunderballs, I mean?"

Nick stared at her. "You? You coach the Thunderballs? Is that what you said, Mom?"

Mom smiled. "That's what I said."

2

"BUT, Mom!" Nick was dumbfounded. "What do you know about coaching? And who ever heard of a woman coaching a baseball team?"

Mom loved baseball just as much as Dad. But only as a spectator. She just *couldn't* mean what she had said.

"I've watched baseball games for more years than I'd care to mention," Mom explained. "And I've seen coaches work too. Particularly your father."

"And I bet Mom can do just as well," Sue put in, shaking back her blond curls.

Her smile showed where she had lost a tooth.

"She just might do better," Dad admitted, beaming.

"She just might," echoed Jen, who had been born between Nick and Sue.

"What have you got to lose?" Dad said. "Without her you might not have a team at all. With her you will."

Nick shrugged. He wasn't exactly elated about the idea. "Well, I guess having a team is better than not having one," he agreed. "Even if we don't win a single game."

"Thanks for the compliment," said Mom.

Nick squeezed out a grin. "I'm sorry, Mom. I really didn't mean that. You sure you want to coach us?"

"Yes, I'm sure. But first you'd better ask

12

your teammates if it's all right with them."

"Wait till tomorrow, Nick," suggested Dad. "This evening you call all the guys and tell them there's practice tomorrow. Tomorrow Mom goes with you to the park and tells the boys she's your new coach. If they don't like it they might as well forget about having a team."

Nick was glum. He had never heard of a woman coach. Never. The guys wouldn't go for it in a million years.

At six o'clock the next afternoon every member of the Thunderballs baseball team was present at the field. So was Mom. Most of the boys knew her. Nick introduced her to the few boys she didn't know.

Mom's talk to the boys was brief. She said that Nick had told her that the Thun-

13

derballs had trouble getting a coach this year, that it was impossible for Mr. Vassey to coach them for a couple of good reasons, and that she had volunteered.

"Some of you might have doubts about my coaching because I'm a woman," she added. "If you do, think of all the women

in positions today whom men had doubts about years ago. And I do happen to know of women coaching basketball and soft-ball. There's no doubt that women are coaching baseball in some other parts of the country." She paused to let that thought sink into their heads a bit. "At least, if I coach, we'll have a team. Isn't it better than not to play at all? Well, what do I hear? Will you accept me as coach? Or won't you?"

There was silence for a second. A long second. It was more like a minute, thought Nick.

"Yes!" said Cyclone Maylor, putting up his hand.

"Yes!" said Jerry Wong. In the next instant every guy there said "Yes" and had his hand in the air.

Mom's face lit up. "Thanks, boys," she said. "From now on you can call me Coach."

Mom wrote the names of each player down on a tablet she had brought with her. After their names she wrote their positions. Then she asked one of the players to hit fly balls to the outfielders and another player to hit to the infielders. There were fourteen players altogether, including two pitchers, Johnny Linn and Frankie Morrow. She had them shag fly balls, too.

Cyclone Maylor and Bill Dakes alternated at second base. Cyclone was hustling and yelling every minute. Bill wasn't. Nick, watching from deep short, felt that Bill wasn't doing his best. Bill hardly made an effort for a ground ball that sizzled past him to the outfield.

"Come on, Bill!" yelled Mom. "Shake a leg out there!"

Bill moved faster after the next one.

Someone laughed nearby. A deep-throated, amused laugh. Nick saw a car parked on the roadside with a man behind the wheel. The car started up and sped down the road.

"Who was that?" asked Mom, curious.

"Burt Stevens," said Russ Gray, the first baseman. "He coaches the Tornadoes, the team that won the pennant the last two years."

"Is that so?" A peculiar light glimmered in Mom's eyes. "Well, maybe by the end of this season he'll laugh out of the other side of his mouth."

A week later Mom made a phone call and scheduled a practice game with — of all teams, thought Nick — the Tornadoes. The game was at six-thirty, Friday.

The Vasseys ate supper early that day. Nick had just finished eating when the Matsons' car pulled up in front of the house. Mrs. Matson was driving and had Gale, Dave and Marge with her.

"Mom, I'm going over to Gale's house

18

for a while," said Nick. "He wants to show me his aquarium."

"Okay," said Mom. "But don't be late for the game."

Gale lived near the edge of Flat Rock. His father, the only black on the police force, used to play professional baseball. He would make a good coach, thought Nick. Too bad he had to work evenings.

The fifteen-gallon aquarium had tropical fish in it — angel fish, black mollies, zebras, neon tetras. Gale pointed the different kinds out with pride while the fish scooted about in all directions.

"Those zebras are devils," he said. "They're always chasing the other fish."

Later they went outdoors. Dave and Marge were skateboarding on the large blacktop driveway in front of the garage. Dave let Nick use his skateboard awhile, and Nick had so much fun he practically forgot about baseball until Mrs. Matson stepped out on the front porch.

"You'd better hurry to your baseball game, boys," she reminded them. "It's almost six-thirty."

"Wow!" cried Nick. "Let's go, Gale! Thanks for letting me skateboard, Dave!"

He and Gale picked up their gloves and hurried to the street. Taking a shortcut through a strawberry field, they arrived at the ball park just as the Thunderball infielders were running out to take their practice.

Jim Rennie was running out to shortstop, Nick's usual position. Nick wondered if Mom was going to let Jim play shortstop even though he, Nick, had gotten to the game in time.

When Nick and Gale ran up, puffing, in

front of the dugout, Mom was handing a ball to Johnny Linn to hit to the infielders. Near first base, Bill Dakes, a utility infielder, was hitting flies to the outfielders.

"Well," Mom said a bit firmly, "I wondered whether you boys had decided to play baseball or go fishing. Nick, work out there with Jim. Gale, trot to the outfield and shag flies with those other boys."

"I'm sorry, Mrs. Vassey," Gale started to apologize. "It was my fault that we —"

"Never mind," Mom interrupted. "Get going. We don't have much time."

Johnny's hits to the infielders were soft and easy to handle. They were nothing like the hard grounders Dad used to hit to them. As far as Nick was concerned, the practice meant nothing more than a little exercise.

Then it was time for the Tornadoes to

take their turn on the field. While they did so Mom reshuffled the lineup slightly.

It was as follows when she was done:

Cyclone Maylor	2b
Jerry Wong	cf
Nick Vassey	ss
Gale Matson	lf
Russ Gray	1b
Wayne Snow	c
Scotty Page	rf
Jim Rennie	3b
Frankie Morrow	p

An umpire of the regular season had accepted the job of umpiring this non-league game. Nick picked up a bat and crouched on one knee in front of the dugout. Waiting for the first pitch from the Tornadoes' tall left-hander, Lefty Burns, was Cyclone Maylor.

Lefty breezed the first pitch by Cyclone for a called strike, then slipped another one by him. Cyclone yanked nervously on his helmet while Mom yelled to him to "swing when it's in there!"

Crack! A high soaring fly to center. The Tornadoes' center fielder moved forward three steps and caught it easily. Jerry Wong socked a grass-cutting grounder down to third for out number two, and Nick was up.

"Here he is!" shouted Bugs Wheeler, the Tornadoes' catcher. "The big one, Lefty!"

And to Nick: "What's your mother been doing, Nick? Taking coaching lessons? Ha!"

Nick glared at Bugs and set his teeth. He watched the first pitch come in, but he was too rattled to be ready for it.

"Strike!" said the ump.

Bugs laughed again. "'Ataway to go, Lefty! Pitch to me, baby! I think I got his number!"

3

NICK braced himself for the next pitch. He tried to forget Bugs's remark, but you can't forget remarks like that very easily.

The pitch. "Ball!"

The next was in there and Nick swung. Crack! A sharp line drive over third! Nick dropped his bat and started to bolt to first base. But he saw the ball curve and strike the ground just inches outside the foul line and he stopped.

"Tough luck, Nick!" shouted Mom.

Bugs was grinning when Nick picked

up the bat to try again. "Too bad, Nick. Maybe your coach could tell you what you did wrong that time."

Shut up! Nick wanted to say. But that would only make Bugs's remarks worse than ever.

"Ball two!"

Lefty couldn't get the next two pitches over either, and Nick walked. He flashed a quick grin at Bugs as he tossed the bat aside. But Bugs wasn't looking at him now.

Gale Matson fouled the first pitch, then drove a sky-rocketing fly to short center field. The shortstop, second baseman and center fielder all ran after it. It was the center fielder who yelled for it and caught it. Three outs.

A pop fly to Nick, a grounder to Jim, and a caught foul tip on the third strike ended the half-inning for the Tornadoes. In the top of the second the Thunderballs picked up their first run, but the Tornadoes put across three on a home run by Bugs with two on. Bugs Wheeler. The guy Nick least wanted to see crack out a homer.

In the top of the third, with one out, Cyclone scored from second on Nick's double. Gale singled, a worm-wiggling grounder that just got by Lefty Burns. Russ Gray walked, filling the bases. Then Wayne Snow hit into a double play, leaving two stranded.

The Tornadoes started to hit Frankie hard in the bottom of the third. They scored a run and still had three men on. Nick looked at Mom sitting in the dugout and wondered why she let Frankie continue pitching. It just proved that she didn't know enough about baseball.

Another run scored and Nick wished now that the Thunderballs had not voted Mom in to coach. She just didn't know what to do at the crucial times, that's all there was to it.

Somehow the Thunderballs got the third out and went to bat, hoping to start a rally of their own. They couldn't. The Tornadoes came back up in the last of the fourth and started where they had left off in the third inning. They were knocking Frankie's pitches all over the lot, and Nick wished he and Gale had stayed away entirely. Mom just was no coach.

And then, after three runs scored and only one out, Mom decided to do something. "Time!" she yelled, running out of the dugout and waving her arms at the umpire. "Johnny! Johnny Linn! Come on!"

"Now we're going to see some strategy!" yelled Bugs Wheeler from the Tornadoes' dugout.

Johnny Linn trotted in from the bullpen where he had been warming up, took the ball from Frankie and stepped onto the mound. He threw a few pitches to Wayne Snow, then stepped off the rubber. The umpire called, "Play ball," and the game resumed.

Nick saw Burt Stevens sitting in the Tornadoes' dugout with a Cheshire-cat grin on his face. Matter of fact, the whole team seemed to be grinning like that. He just could not understand why Mom got a practice game with them when there were weaker teams in the league. She just could not have been thinking.

Johnny Linn got the next two men out without letting the Tornadoes score. But the Tornadoes picked up three more runs during the next two innings to the Thunderballs' two and won the game 11 to 4.

"Better luck next time, Coach!" Coach Stevens yelled over at Mom, the cat grin on his face.

Mom smiled back. "We're not worrying, Mr. Stevens! The real fight has not yet begun!"

Nick stared at her. *What* was she saying? Wasn't it enough that she was a woman without saying a thing like that?

The next day Jerry Wong came over with Scotty and took turns playing chess with Nick. Jerry's father ran the only Chinese-American restaurant in Flat Rock.

Next to baseball, Nick liked chess best.

29

Matter of fact, now that Mom was coaching he probably liked chess better.

Nick won once, Scotty once, and Jerry twice. In both of Jerry's games his queen and rook tied up his opponent's king so quickly that the guys hardly knew what had happened.

After their chess games the next day, they went outdoors to skateboard. Most of the kids in the neighborhood skateboarded at one time or another on the sidewalks. Even Jen and Sue had skateboards of their own.

"Nick, look!"

Nick swung around at Jen's voice, almost losing his balance and falling off the skateboard. There was Jerry Wong on his skateboard, standing on his hands. The guys and girls looked at him as if transfixed.

"Hey!" Nick said. "You practicing for some show or something?"

Jerry grinned at him. "No. I just learned this yesterday."

A chess hotshot, now a skateboard hotshot, thought Nick. What was the guy going to do next?

"Hah!" smirked Scotty. "He's just showing off for the girls."

That did it. Jerry got off the board and on it with his feet.

"You lunkhead," snapped Jen. "You embarrassed him."

"I didn't mean to," apologized Scotty.

Jerry was smiling, however, his face red from having stood on his hands. It was hard to tell whether he was embarrassed or not. But he wasn't sore. That was the important thing. He was sensitive, but seldom had Nick seen him sore.

The boys rode down the sidewalk and started to turn past the corner drugstore when something in the field across Columbus Street caught their attention. A boy was riding a shiny black horse, sitting straight on its bare back while it trotted as hard as it probably could. The boy was Wayne Snow. He looked at the guys for an instant, and then looked away.

Scotty sighed. "Well, la de da!" he sang. "Isn't it nice to be rich? You can pretend you don't know the guys you play baseball with."

Down the highway a bit was a big white house where Wayne lived with his parents. When they were home, that is. Otherwise there was no one except him, his older brother Ron, and a housekeeper. Mrs. Snow was always traipsing about the country putting on fashion shows, and Mr.

33

Snow was usually away on a business trip. Nick didn't know exactly what he did.

Just then two kids on skateboards rounded the corner a block away and started up the sidewalk toward the boys.

"Hey, look who's there!" one of them shouted. "Nick, I heard your Mom's coaching the Thunderballs!"

Jabber Kane was one kid with the perfect nickname.

"So what?" said Nick. The kid with Jabber was Steve Dale. Both boys played with the Clowns.

Jabber laughed as they approached. "Who ever heard of a woman coaching a boys' baseball team?"

"What difference does it make?" snapped Nick. "She probably knows more about baseball than your whole bunch of Clowns put together."

Jabber's wide smile showed large teeth

in front, teeth that Nick felt like knocking down Jabber's skinny throat.

"I can't wait till we play you guys," said Jabber. "I can picture your Mom yelling from the dugout, 'Come on, boys! Don't slide unless you have to! You mustn't get your pants dirty!' Ha!"

The guys laughed. Including Scotty and Jerry. Nick saw red. He squared his jaw and went after Jabber, his fists clenched. Jabber whisked around on his skateboard and sped off down the sidewalk, his laughter trailing after him.

"Forget it," said Scotty. "He's only kidding."

"I know," replied Nick. "But I don't like it. I hope that when we play those Clowns we'll beat them twenty to nothing."

What he really wished, though, was that someone else were coaching the Thunderballs. Someone else, not Mom.

4

"MAKE a lot of noise out there," Mom told the boys. "Let Johnny know he has nothing to worry about."

With that final order from the coach, the Thunderballs ran out on the field. It was July 5, the Thunderballs' first game of the season. At bat were the Knicks, a scrappy bunch of guys who were talking it up loudly in and around their dugout as if they had the game sewn up already.

Johnny Linn, on the mound for the Thunderballs, threw in several warm-up pitches to Wayne. The umpire yelled

"Play ball!" and the Knicks' first hitter stepped to the plate. He was short and his suit was almost too big for him.

"Ball!" cried the ump, as Johnny's first pitch zipped high over the plate.

The infield chatter grew louder but it didn't help Johnny's control. He walked the batter. The next man bunted down to first. Johnny threw him out but the other runner was safe on second.

The next man lined a single over short, scoring the runner.

"Just lucky, Johnny," Nick said. He caught the throw-in from left fielder Gale Matson and tossed it to Johnny. "Let's go for two."

The Knicks' batter socked a bouncing grounder to short. Nick caught it and whipped it to second. Cyclone caught it, snapped it to first. A double play!

"There you go!" smiled Nick.

"You asked for it," Johnny smiled back at him.

"Cyclone Maylor! Jerry Wong! Nick Vassey!" Mom read off the names of the first three hitters. "Let's get that run back!"

Cyclone let two strikes go past him, then socked a cloud-high drive above the pitcher's mound. The Knicks' third baseman took it for the first out. Jerry let a strike go by, then took four straight balls for a free pass to first. Nick came up, looked over a couple, then hit a slow grounder to third. The third baseman fielded it, looked toward second, saw that he couldn't get Jerry, and threw to first. Out.

Gale pounded a long fly to center. Three away.

The Knicks came up, eager to pile up runs. But they didn't get any. Instead it was the Thunderballs who began popping the ball in between the Knicks. Russell Gray started it off with a single, followed by Wayne Snow's hot grounder over the third-base bag. Scotty Page drove a long fly to right which was caught, but which advanced Russ to third.

"Only one out!" yelled Mom, standing in front of the dugout with a finger jabbing the air. "Play it safe!"

"Thataway to talk to 'em, Coach!" a fan yelled from the stands. Other fans made remarks, too. They were sure getting a big kick out of seeing a woman coach a base-ball team.

The remarks embarrassed Nick as he stood in the third-base coaching box. The people were having a good time, all right. But it was mostly over watching and listening to Mom. The game had little to do with it. That was how it seemed anyway.

Pat Krupa singled, driving in Russ. Wayne advanced all around to third. Then Johnny Linn singled to left, scoring Wayne. The fans stood up and clapped their hands thunderously, particularly the young fans. Jen and Sue were with a bunch of girls and they were shouting louder than ever.

The lead-off man, Cyclone, was up again. Monk Jones, the Knicks' tall right-hander, breezed a third strike by him for the Thunderballs' second out. Then Jerry popped up to the catcher, ending the rally and the bottom of the second inning.

Mom patted Johnny's back as he started out of the dugout. "Keep your pitches in there, Johnny," she said. "You've got good boys behind you."

Johnny simply nodded. He was a quiet kid. A half-dozen words from him equaled a thousand from Cyclone.

The Knicks started to hit. A double over second base. A single between third and short. A long fly to second which Jerry caught, but which accounted for a run after the runner tagged up. Two more runs scored before the Thunderballs could settle down and make the second and third outs.

Knicks 4 — Thunderballs 2.

It was the Knicks fans' turn to yell now. "How do you like them apples, Coach Vassey?" one of them said.

"That's right," Wayne said softly. "That's just the beginning."

Nick stared at him. "That's a fine thing to say, Wayne."

Mom, standing nearby, smiled. "That's being a defeatist, Wayne. We won't win if you feel that way."

Wayne's face turned beet red.

5

NICK led off in the bottom of the third.

"A home run, Nick!" Jen yelled in that soprano voice of hers. "Over the fence!"

Monk Jones rubbed the ball, nodded with satisfaction at the signal from his catcher, then stretched and delivered. Nick pulled back his bat, saw that the pitch was going wide and held his swing.

"Ball!" yelled the ump.

Monk drilled the next pitch across the inside corner for a strike. Nick cut at the next one and heard the ball plop into the catcher's mitt.

"He's your man, Monk, ol' boy!" shouted the Knicks' catcher.

Nick stepped out of the box, rubbed the bat gingerly, and looked at Monk. Monk might try to fool him with a curve this time. He stepped back into the box.

The pitch came in close, then curved away. Nick swung. *Crack!* The ball struck the ground in front of Monk, bounced high over his head and then over second base for a single. The fans yelled as Nick stood on the bag at first and looked at Mom for a bunt signal. But she gave none.

Gale, up next, blasted the first pitch in a line drive over second. Nick swept around second base and headed for third.

"Go! Go! Go!" third-base coach Tom

Warren shouted, swinging his left arm like a windmill.

Nick rounded third and raced for home. As he got close to it he heard Mom and some of the guys yelling to him, "Hit it, Nick! Hit the dirt!"

Nick did. The catcher caught the relay and put it on Nick, but Nick was already across the plate. "Safe!" cried the ump.

Nick got up, brushed off his pants and saw Gale trotting back to second base for a clean double. "Nice running, Nick," Mom said. "Okay, Russ! Let's keep it going!"

Russell Gray fouled the first two pitches to the backstop screen, let an inside pitch go by, then went down swinging. Next batter was Wayne Snow. He walked to the plate, dragging his bat over the ground.

"Look at him," muttered Scotty disgust-

45

edly. "How are we going to win with him acting like that?"

"Liven up, Wayne!" snapped Cyclone. "This is a ball game, not a funeral!"

"All right, all right," cautioned Mom. "Cut out the remarks."

Wayne swung at a high pitch and drove it in a line over the fence. It went foul. He

swung at the next pitch and sent it a mile
into the sky. This one dropped behind the
home-plate stands.

"Straighten it out, Wayne!" Mom
shouted.

There was a chuckle in the stands and
Nick looked over at Mom. Either she had
not heard it or she wasn't letting on she

had. Her shout did sound funny, though, coming from the dugout. After thinking about it, he felt a funny sensation — a sensation of pride. It took a lot of nerve to do what Mom was doing.

Monk's next three pitches were balls. Then Wayne stepped into a sidearm pitch, swung hard, and missed completely. He walked back to the dugout, dragging the bat, not looking anywhere except at the ground.

"Forget it, Wayne," said Mom. "You'll be up again."

Scotty waited out Monk's pitches and got a free ticket to first. Pat came up, took two balls and a strike, then laced a drive to deep center field. It sure looked as if it were heading for the Great Beyond. But the Knicks' center fielder, running back as hard as he could, reached up his gloved hand and nabbed it.

The Knicks came up and put across two more runs to give them a 6 to 3 lead. With two on and two out the Knicks' batter drove a hot liner directly at Nick. It was high. Nick leaped, stretching as far as he could. *Pop!* He had it!

He ran in from short, sweat dripping off his face. A few inches higher and that ball would have gone over his head and two more runs would have scored.

He looked sorrowfully at Mom. Her first game, he thought, and they were going to lose it. She caught his eye and smiled.

I don't know, he thought. We're losing the game and she looks as happy as if we were winning it. If Dad were in her place, *he* wouldn't be smiling. You could bet your life on that.

49

6

JOHNNY LINN led off in the bottom of the fourth inning with a colossal triple to left center field. It sure looked like a good start. But Bill Dakes, batting for Cyclone, grounded out to third and Jerry Wong bounced one back to the pitcher for the second out.

"Oh, no!" Mom moaned. "Jim, bat for Nick! Wait for a good one! Tom, get ready to bat for Gale."

Nick tossed his bat onto the pile fanned out on the ground and returned to the

50

dugout. He wasn't happy about being replaced, but he knew that Mom wanted every player on the team to play at least three innings. It was a league rule that every player had to play at least two innings. Mom preferred to be a little more generous whenever she could.

Jim Rennie drew a walk. Then Tom Warren walked, filling the bases!

The Thunderballs' dugout livened up like a beehive. "A grand slammer, Russ!" yelled Nick. "Clean the bases!"

Russ wiggled the toes of his sneakers into the soft, dusty earth, tugged at his protective helmet, then got ready for Monk's pitch. The ball came in slightly high. Russ swung, and missed.

"Too high, Russ!" Cyclone shouted.

The next was high, too. Again he swung and missed. The Thunderball fans groaned. Monk pitched another high one. This one Russ let go by. Ball one.

Monk threw two more balls for a three-two count, then rifled the next one in knee-high. Russ swung hard and missed for strike three. Three away. Russ tossed his bat angrily toward the dugout and ran out to his position at first base. Nick knew exactly how he felt. He had struck out with the bases loaded a few times himself.

"Scotty," said Mom, as Scotty started out of the dugout, "wait. Mike, take right field."

"Yes, sir," said Mike Todey. "I mean, yes, ma'am."

Nick grinned. Guess it was going to be a long while before most of the boys would be calling Mom "Coach."

The Knicks picked up a run in the top of the fifth with a double and then an error by Jim Rennie. He had made a neat catch on a fast bouncing ball, but pegged it too high to first base. The runner on second scored on the overthrow. The run was the only one the Knicks got.

The Thunderballs started off like a straw fire during their turn at bat. Wayne Snow belted a hot grounder that zipped over the third-base bag for a double. Mike Todey singled him in and Pat Krupa drew a pass.

"Look at Pat," said Scotty. "He wobbles like a duck. I can't see how he can run as fast as he does."

"He pulls back all levers and goes when he has to," Nick said, grinning.

Johnny Linn, up next, also drew a walk, filling the bases. Again the Thunderballs' fans grew excited and began to yell for a hit. Any kind of hit.

Bill Dakes tapped the tip of his bat against the plate, lifted it to his shoulder, and waited for the pitch. It was high. Ball one. He swung at the next pitch and laced it to left field. The fielder hardly had to move. Mike Todey, on third, stayed on the bag until the ball was caught, then bolted for home. He made it easily.

Jerry Wong took a called strike, then belted a searing grounder directly at the shortstop. The guy fielded it, snapped it to second. Second to first. A double play. Three outs.

"We picked up two, anyway," said Mom. "Now get out there and hold them."

Hold them they did. Johnny struck out the first man and the next two grounded out. The Thunderballs came up for the last time. They were trailing 7 to 5. Fat chance they had of winning this ball game thought Nick. It would have been a good start to have won the first league game for Mom.

Jim Rennie led off and smashed the second pitch for a clean single over second. Then Tom Warren popped out to put a damper on the Thunderballs' hopes of getting a run. Russ, having struck out the last two times at bat, didn't raise anyone's hopes as he strode to the plate. He took a called strike, a ball, then hammered a solid drive to right center field! Jim raced all around to home and Russ took second on the play on Jim.

Wayne went down swinging. Two away. And two runs from winning the ball game. It still seemed hopeless.

Then Mike walked. Pat hit a grounder to short. It was fumbled! Russ held up at third, Mike at second. Pat was on first. The tying run — and the winning run — were on base!

"Win your own ball game, Johnny!"

yelled a fan. "Chase home those ducks!"

Johnny Linn waited out the pitches. Then, with the count two and two, he swung at a chest-high pitch. *Crack!* A line drive over the shortstop's head! Russ scored. Mike scored. Pat halted on third, leaving Johnny with a double.

The game was over. The Thunderballs were the winners, 8 to 7. Mom had won her first league ball game.

7

TWO days later the Thunderballs tangled with the Zebras. Mom had Bill Dakes and Jim Rennie start in place of Cyclone and Nick. The Thunderballs had first raps, but in the first two innings they could do little against their opponents. Eddie Cash, the Zebras' little right-hander, didn't seem to have much on the ball, yet no Thunderball could hit him.

Frankie Morrow, pitching for the Thunderballs, was tagged for four hits and three runs in the two innings. He led off the third with a single, though, and Bill sacrificed him to second on a bunt. Then Jerry Wong tripled, scoring Frankie, and Jim hit a high fly which landed between three fielders for a freak double, scoring Jerry. It was funny the way the three Zebras stood there, each expecting the other to catch the ball.

"Remember that incident," Mom said. "If that ever happens to you, *someone call for the ball*. Don't let it drop between you."

The two runs were all the Thunderballs scored that half-inning. In the top of the fourth Mike Todey, batting for Scotty Page, walked. Then Gale, pinch-hitting for Pat Krupa, walloped a home run over the left-field fence. Two singles and an error accounted for another run and the Thunderballs went into the lead, 5 to 3.

Nick smiled as he trotted out to short,

replacing Jim Rennie. It looked as if Mom's Thunderballs were heading for their second straight victory.

The Zebras squeezed in a run in the bottom of the fourth, but the Thunderballs got it back in the fifth. And then, in the bottom of the fifth, the Zebras pulled out all stops and really poured it on the Thunderballs. They collected five hits and four runs for a total of eight runs. The Thunderballs drew a goose egg in the sixth and that was it. The Zebras won 8 to 6.

"Well," Mom said, heaving a sigh, "we can't win them all."

"We were just lucky to win the first one," muttered Wayne Snow.

Mom stared at him. "Lucky, did you say?"

Wayne's face turned cherry red. "Well, maybe we weren't."

He climbed out of the dugout, picked up the catcher's mitt and shoved it inside the canvas bag where the other baseball equipment was kept. Then he hung around, cleaning his fingernails, while the color of his face gradually returned to normal.

Mom looked at Wayne as if trying to figure him out. She told the boys to put the bats and balls into the bag and then put the bag into her car.

"Come on, Wayne," Mom said, when they were ready to leave. "You can ride with us as far as our house."

He seemed reluctant at first. Then he shrugged and got into the car. Nick thought that Mom would say something more to Wayne, but she didn't. And he was glad. Wayne looked as if he didn't care to talk about anything.

Wayne helped Nick lift the equipment

out of the car when they reached home. Wayne spotted the tent Dad had put in the yard for Nick. "That's a beauty. Ever spend a night in it?"

"Oh, sure," said Nick. He met Wayne's eyes. "Wayne, you're not very happy about my mother's coaching us, are you?"

Wayne's lips twitched. "I didn't say anything."

"No. But that's what you're thinking, isn't it? I'm not too keen about it, either. And some of the other guys feel the same way. But nobody else will coach us. If she didn't coach us we wouldn't have a team. Did you ask your Dad if he'd like to coach us?"

Wayne didn't answer for a while. At last he said, "Your mother's okay. I'm just not crazy about baseball. I've even thought of quitting. I don't know. Maybe I will or maybe I won't."

He walked away. When he was halfway to the sidewalk he turned and said over his shoulder, "So long. And thanks for the ride."

Nick frowned after him. Wayne quitting? Did he really mean it? He really was a strange kid. Why hadn't he answered those questions about his father? What did his father do that made him unable to coach the team? Was it because he didn't know enough about baseball? Or was it some other reason?

Nick went into the house and saw that Dad was home. He certainly was putting in some long hours lately.

"Dad, do you know Mr. Snow? Know what his job is?"

Dad shrugged. "He's an importer, I think. Brings goods in from abroad. Why?"

"Wayne never talks about him."

"Maybe Wayne doesn't know exactly what he does," answered Dad.

It sure seemed funny. *He* knew what *his* dad did.

On Saturday afternoon Gale and Scotty came over and the three of them rode their skateboards down to the corner. They stopped in the drugstore for ice-cream cones and rode on the sidewalk on Columbus Street till they were opposite Wayne Snow's house.

Nick heard sharp, cracking sounds coming from the place, and saw baseballs flying through the air on the other side of the garage.

"How do you like that?" he said. "He's practicing batting! And the other day he said he didn't like baseball!"

8

THE boys picked up their skateboards and walked over to the other side of the garage.

Johnny Linn, with a half a dozen baseballs at his feet, was pitching them in to Wayne who was standing with his back to the garage.

"Hi!" greeted Nick. "Getting in some practice?"

"Hi," said Johnny.

"Hi," said Wayne, and shrugged. "I need it, don't I?"

"Thought you said you might quit baseball," said Nick. "You wouldn't do this if you were going to quit, would you?"

Wayne shrugged. "I said it because I can't hit. Then Johnny said he was willing to pitch to me."

"He said I could ride his horse," Johnny said.

"Let's quit." Wayne tossed his bat to the ground. "I've had enough, anyway."

Nick noticed a swimming pool to the left of the garage, encircled by a high wire fence. There was a small, child-size row-boat in the pool with oars inside it. There were several canvas lounging chairs and a sun umbrella, folded down over a table, along the side of the pool.

This Wayne kid has everything, thought Nick. And what he didn't have, he prob-ably could get. All he had to do was ask for it. What a life!

A car turned into the driveway. A long black sports car so clean and shiny you could see your reflection in it. It stopped and a young man in slacks and a sporty sweater hopped out of it.

"Hi, gang," he greeted cheerfully, and looked at Wayne. "Sorry to bust up your

fun, brother, but we're driving up to the cottage."

Wayne frowned. "Now?"

"Now. Get Mrs. Lane to pack your clothes. Make sure there's enough for two weeks."

"*Two weeks?*"

"Two weeks," repeated his big brother. "Come on. Let's go." He bounded to the house in his white sneakers. Probably, thought Nick, they had a tennis court next to their cottage. And if the cottage was beside a lake they probably had a boat, too.

"Your mother and father, are they at the cottage?" Nick asked.

"Just my mother," replied Wayne. "She went there —" he faltered and swallowed. "Well, she's been away a couple of days on that business she's got with dresses and stuff and went to the cottage when she got through. Dad's going there later."

He didn't seem impressed about going at all.

"Wayne!" shouted his brother from the side porch of the house. "Are you coming or aren't you?"

"I'm coming," said Wayne, not enthusiastically. "Nick, will you tell your mother that I won't be at the games for the next couple of weeks? I hope she won't have trouble getting somebody to catch."

"I'll tell her," said Nick.

Suddenly he thought: Who else *could* catch for the Thunderballs? Boy! Mom's headaches in coaching a Little League baseball team were just beginning!

9

"I THINK you're the man to do it," Mom announced after she and Nick had talked about the catching position for a while. "You're strong and you have a good arm. A good arm's a major ingredient for a catcher, isn't it?"

"Yes, but I've never caught before, Mom. I don't know anything about signals."

"One finger's for a straight ball, two fingers for a hook," explained Mom. "You don't have to worry about that anyway.

Johnny will be pitching against the Tornadoes. He knows the batters pretty well. If he doesn't like what you're calling for he'll shake it off."

She smiled as she said it, as if Johnny Linn were a big-leaguer or something. He didn't say any more. Fact was, he could not think of anyone else on the team who had caught before either. And Wayne was going to be gone for two weeks. That meant that Nick would have to catch about four games.

Jim Rennie, who was going to play shortstop, was a weak infielder, too. So there were two positions which had been weakened because of Wayne's not playing. Nick shook his head sadly. He could see the Thunderballs coming out on the tail end of the next three or four games.

Poor Mom! She probably will wish she

had not volunteered to take on a coaching job.

Burt Stevens, the Tornadoes' coach, hit hard grounders to his infielders and kept them hustling every minute. Nick knew what he must be thinking. Mr. Stevens had won the pennant the last two years and he wasn't going to let a woman coach stop him from winning it again this year.

The Tornadoes, batting first, got on to Johnny's pitching almost immediately. They chalked up two runs before the Thunderballs could get them out.

"That's the way we'll be getting them!" Bugs Wheeler yelled loud enough for everybody to hear. "Two runs at a time!"

Nick felt his neck burn. How he hoped he could make Bugs eat those words!

Bill Dakes walked and Jerry Wong singled to get them off to a good start. But
Nick hit into a double play, and Tom Warren flied out to left, ending the half-inning
without a run.

In the top of the second the Tornadoes
didn't score either.

"Where are those two runs, Bugs?" Nick
yelled across the diamond.

"We'll make it up the next time!" Bugs
yelled back.

The Thunderballs picked up one run on
Mike's single and a triple by Pat Krupa.
The Tornadoes came back with a run in
the top of the third. But it was only one
run, not two. And then there was a shout
from one of the guys and Nick saw Wayne
Snow come trotting around the corner of
the dugout.

"Wayne!" he shouted, followed by a

similar chorus from the other guys. "Am I glad to see you!"

Wayne was in uniform, ready to play. His face beamed. "My brother drove me down," he explained. "He's going to do it every time we have a game. He doesn't mind. It's only sixty miles to our cottage."

Only sixty miles, thought Nick. Ron probably covered it in no time in that sports car of his.

"I'm glad to see you, too, Wayne," said Mom. "When this half-inning's over, take over the catching job from Nick. I'm sure he won't mind." She looked from Nick to Jim, as if trying to decide which to let play shortstop. Then she said, "Jim, let Nick take over short, will you?"

"Sure, Coach," Jim said.

Nick knew that making a decision between him and Jim was tough. Mom didn't want anyone to feel that she was favoring him. But in this game, it seemed best that he play.

Bill Dakes led off with a single over second and Jerry advanced him to third on a double to left center field. It seemed that their hitting streak ended right there, for Nick grounded out to first and Tom Warren fanned. Then Russ walked, loading the bases.

"You want Wayne to bat for me?" Jim asked Mom. He had his helmet on, ready to go to the plate.

"With the bases filled?" Mom smiled. "No, Jim. You get up there and hit the ball. Drive in those runs."

Jim walked to the plate, settled his helmet better on his head, and waited for the pitch from Bob Kreel, the Tornadoes' tall right-hander.

"Strike one!" yelled the ump as Bob breezed the ball past Jim.

The next was a ball. So was the next. Then Jim tagged one. A long high fly toward the left-field fence. The Tornadoes' outfielder ran back after it but it was no use. It went over the fence for a grand-slam homer.

Everyone, including Mom, stepped out of the dugout and shook Jim's hand as he trotted in. And the Thunderballs' fans yelled as they had never yelled before. Mike flied out, ending the rally. Tornadoes 3 — Thunderballs 5.

Then the Tornadoes started rolling. They didn't stop until they had collected three runs, surging ahead of the Thunderballs 6 to 5.

"Hey, Thunderballs! We're just kidding with you!" yelled a Tornado sitting on the bench. "Watch what happens the next two innings!"

"You watch, too!" snorted Gale. "Because you're not going to do anything!"

Mom smiled at him. "Thataway, Gale. Let's show them that *we're* not kidding."

10

CYCLONE batted for Pat in the bottom of the fourth and slammed a two-one pitch to deep center. It looked good until the center fielder reached up his gloved hand and pulled it out of the air.

Johnny Linn grounded out on the first pitch and Bill Dakes flied out to right. It was a fast half-inning.

The Tornadoes connected with two clean hits through the infield. Then Nick made a nice stop at short and threw the ball to Bill to start a double play. Too wide! One run scored! Scotty Page, who had taken Mike's place in right field, retrieved the ball and pegged it in.

Nick tightened his lips with disgust. He had been too hasty and not careful. There were still two men on — one on first, the other on third. "C'mon, Johnny! C'mon, kid! They won't do it again, Johnny!"

A long fly to deep center. Jerry Wong caught it, pegged it in. Bill caught the peg and relayed it home, but not in time. The runner had tagged up at third and scored. Johnny fanned the next two batters to retire the side. But the Tornadoes had chalked up two runs to boost their total to 8.

Jerry, leading off in the bottom of the fifth, received a nice ovation as he strode to the plate. That was a good catch he had made in center field. He took a called strike, a ball, then belted a hard grounder through the pitcher's box for a single. Nick, up next, socked a hard grounder to second. The second baseman fumbled it and Nick was safe at first, Jerry safe at second.

Gale, batting for Tom Warren, blasted a double between left and center, scoring Jerry. But the fielder retrieved the ball quickly and the coach held Nick up at third.

No outs so far. Nick wished that somebody would hit him in. But Russ struck out, Wayne popped to short, and Scotty flied to left. Dismally Nick shook his head, picked up his glove and ran out to his position.

In the top of the sixth the Tornadoes picked up another run to help make their lead more secure — 9 to 6. It was the Thunderballs' last chance at bat. Their last chance to overtake the Tornadoes.

The Thunderballs' bench was silent as

Cyclone put on his helmet, picked up his bat and went to the plate.

"What is this?" said Mom. "A funeral wake? Let's hear some chatter. Come on. Liven up!"

Across the way, on the Tornadoes' bench, Nick saw a smug look on Coach Stevens's face, as if the coach was having the time of his life. If only the Thunderballs could do something to wipe that smile off, thought Nick. If only *he* could do something. But he was fifth to bat and might not get his chance.

The first pitch to Cyclone. He swung. A single over short! Then Johnny belted a low pitch that glanced off the pitcher's left foot and sailed through the space between first and second. Bill Dakes hit a grounder to the shortstop's right side. The shortstop fielded it and threw to second, getting out Johnny. The second baseman pegged to first to try for a double play, but Bill Dakes beat the throw by a step. One away, runners on first and third.

The Thunderballs' fans were roaring now. "Keep it up, Jerry!" one of them yelled. "Let's turn this game upside down!"

Nick, on one knee in front of the dugout, hoped Jerry would get a hit. A double play would end the game, and Nick wanted so much to bat again and have a chance to wipe that smug look off Coach Stevens's face.

Bob Kreel stretched, delivered. Ball one. The next was a strike. Then Jerry swung at a high one and popped it up. Two outs. Winning sure looked impossible.

"Tag it, Nick," said Gale. "Save me a rap."

Nick tugged at his helmet and stepped to the plate. Bob Kreel stretched, pitched. "Strike!" yelled the ump.

Then, "Strike two!" Nick stepped out of the box and glanced at the umpire. He didn't like that call but he said nothing.

"Ball!"

One and two was the count. The next pitch came in and Nick swung. *Crack!* A long, high fly heading for the left-field fence! The fielder ran back . . . back . . . Over the fence it went! A home run!

Nick circled the bases, a grin on his face as he crossed the plate. The whole gang, including Mom, stood outside the dugout and shook his hand.

"It's all tied up!" Mom exclaimed. "One more run to go!"

"There you are, Gale!" smiled Nick.

Gale grinned. "Thanks, Nick." He took

a called strike, then smashed a searing double to left field!

Russ Gray was next up to bat.

"Drive him in, Russ!" yelled Mom. "A single will do it!"

Bob Kreel took his time. He threw nothing good in his first three pitches. Then he poured in a strike, then another for a three-two count. His next was good, too. Russ belted it. A clean single over short! Gale scored and the game was over. Thunderballs 10 — Tornadoes 9.

Coach Stevens came over and shook Mom's hand. "Congratulations, Coach," he said, smiling broadly. "You came through like a veteran."

Mom smiled pleasantly. "Thank you, Coach. Maybe we were a little . . . lucky?"

Nick felt that Mom was really enjoying

the moment, paying back Coach Stevens a little of the needling he and his team had been giving her and the Thunderballs.

Coach Stevens cleared his throat. "Well, I can't say that. Your boys were hitting very well toward the end. But don't worry," he added, chuckling, "you don't think for a minute that I'm going to let a woman beat me out of another pennant, do you?"

Mom shrugged as if the idea had not occurred to her before. "It would be something to remember, wouldn't it?" she said.

11

A THOUGHT occurred to Nick right after dinner the next day. It was a hot, sticky night. Nobody was home at the Snows. Nobody would know . . .

"Hey, guys," he said to Gale and Scotty when they came over. "Let's go swimming in Wayne Snow's swimming pool. Nobody's home there. Why let that big beautiful pool go to waste?"

"How about their housekeeper?" questioned Scotty. "Isn't she there?"

"She lives in her own home. She wouldn't be there now." The idea became better and better all the time.

"Wayne's a funny guy," Gale said doubtfully. "Think he'd get sore at us if he found out?"

"Who's going to tell him?" said Nick.

Gale and Scotty looked at each other, then both shrugged. "Guess it's all right," said Gale.

"Why not?" said Scotty. "We're not going to hurt the water, are we? Even if Wayne does find out, he wouldn't care."

"Let's go!" cried Nick, so pleased with the idea he couldn't wait to get to the pool.

Each boy picked up his swimming trunks at his house. They met at the Snows' house and changed into their trunks on the back porch. The gate was locked, so they climbed over the wire fence to the pool.

The boys dived in and swam from one end of the pool to the other. Then they ducked each other and laughed, having the time of their lives. The water was warm, perfect.

Nick didn't know how long they had been in the pool — fifteen minutes . . . maybe twenty — when he saw that Gale suddenly had stopped swimming and was looking at something, or *someone*, beyond the pool. Nick followed his friend's gaze and then froze.

A tall, lean-faced man in a light gray suit and wearing a narrow-brimmed hat stood there on the other side of the fence, looking at them. He was smiling, but his smile wasn't warm enough to ease Nick's panic. They were caught swimming in the pool, in a private pool where they had no business being. That was all Nick could think about at the moment.

"Hi," the man greeted them in a voice so polite it surprised Nick. "How's the water?"

Nick stared at Gale, then saw Scotty pop out of the water a yard or so to his left. "F-fine!" he stuttered.

He swam to the edge and climbed out. Gale and Scotty started to follow him.

"You don't have to get out," said the man. "I'm Mr. Snow. I think I've seen you boys in the neighborhood, haven't I?"

Nick forced a smile. It was possible that Mr. Snow had seen them, but this was the first time he had ever seen Mr. Snow.

"We live just a few blocks away," admitted Nick, grabbing up a towel and drying himself. *You're not supposed to be here, Mr. Snow!* he wanted to yell. *You're supposed to be going to your cottage. That's where your wife is. And Ron and Wayne.*

You're not supposed to catch us swimming in your pool!

That's what hurt him, getting caught swimming in the pool. Now he knew how terribly wrong it was. And it had seemed such a good idea.

He looked at Gale and Scotty. They were drying themselves, too. And looking ashamed.

"I — I'm sorry, Mr. Snow," said Nick. "This was my idea."

"I'm sorry, too, Mr. Snow," said Gale.

"So am I," said Scotty.

A small peal of laughter bubbled from Mr. Snow. "You've repented! That's good enough for me!" He waved to them. "Well, I'm on my way to our cottage to see the rest of my family. I wanted to stop here to drop off some of my work. So long, boys."

"So long, Mr. Snow." They said it almost together.

They were dressed by the time they heard Mr. Snow's car backing out of the driveway. "He's not a bad guy at all, is he?" said Nick, as he heard the car gun up the street.

"No, he isn't," said Gale. "And for that reason I'm sorrier for going into the pool than I would be if he was."

They climbed over the fence and started down the street.

"Race you to the corner," said Nick numbly.

He didn't feel like racing, though. He just wanted to say something to break the awful silence.

The Thunderballs beat the Clowns on Friday. Wayne's brother Ron had driven him to the game and Mom thanked them both.

Then Nick asked Wayne if his father

had told him about the swimming pool incident. "No," said Wayne, looking surprised. "What happened?"

"Nothing, except that Gale, Scotty and I went swimming in it and your dad caught us. We told him we were sorry."

Wayne smiled. "That's okay," he said. "Come over anytime."

"Not unless you're there," replied Nick, shaking his head. Under no circumstances would he ever go there again unless one of the Snows was home. Not only was it dangerous to swim in an unsupervised pool, but it was outright trespassing.

On Tuesday the Thunderballs rolled over the Knicks, knocking Monk Jones out of the box in the third inning. Mom was especially pleased about that.

On Thursday something unusual took place just before the game with the Zebras.

94

A photographer from the local paper, the Flat Rock *Sentinel,* arrived. With him was a reporter who asked Mom all sorts of questions about herself, her family, when her interest in baseball had begun and so on. The photographer took pictures of her and stayed for the game.

The Thunderballs scored twice in the third, twice in the fourth, and once in the sixth. The Zebras piled up only three runs altogether, and lost the ball game 5 to 3.

"Things weren't looking so good in the first two innings," said Cyclone as the team was loading the equipment into the car. "Those newspaper guys must have brought us good luck."

"It wasn't luck," said Mom. "You boys are getting good."

Mom, Dad, Nick and the girls went to Wong's Chinese-American Restaurant for dinner the next evening. Mr. Wong, Jerry's father, came to their table to wait on them.

"Congratulations, Mrs. Vassey," he said. "Nice picture of you in the paper. Fine write-up, too."

"Thank you, Mr. Wong," said Mom, smiling modestly.

"Well, hi, Coach," said a voice from the other side of the room. "Heard the Zebras did some sloppy playing yesterday."

All eyes turned and settled on Coach Burt Stevens sitting there with his entire family. Mrs. Stevens, the coach, and their two children began to laugh.

"Hi, Coach Stevens," greeted Mom. "Yes, we won. I thought the Thunderballs did some fine playing."

"Remember what I said before," said Coach Stevens with a chuckle. "There's still a long way to go."

Dad took a pencil and a small pad out of his pocket, wrote on the pad, tore out the sheet and folded it. When a waitress brought the food Dad handed her the sheet. "Give this to Mr. Stevens, will you, please?"

"Certainly." She took the note to Mr. Stevens who read it, then burst out laughing.

"You're on, Craig!" he said to Dad.

Everyone looked curiously from him to Dad. "What's that all about?" asked Mom curiously.

Dad grinned. "A private secret between Burt and me. Let's eat."

12

THE GAME Nick had dreaded was with the Tornadoes on Wednesday, July 27. He didn't like that smirk on Mr. Stevens's face. He didn't like Bugs Wheeler's sarcastic remarks. Matter of fact, he didn't like the Tornadoes at all.

"Let's beat these guys," he said as he squeezed in between Gale and Johnny on the bench. "We whipped them before. Let's do it again."

He wasn't starting at short. Jim Rennie was. That meant that he would go in for the last two or three innings.

"Bill, Jerry, Jim," Mom read off the

names of the first three hitters. "Pick up your bats. Get up there and swing."

The Thunderballs had first raps. Lefty Burns was pitching for the Tornadoes, looking tall and confident on the mound. He got two strikes on Bill, then Bill laced a grounder through short for a single, and went to second on Jerry's sacrifice bunt.

Jim flied out. Then Tom Warren doubled, scoring Bill, and Mike Todey singled, scoring Tom. Wayne flied out for the third out.

"Nice start, guys!" cried Nick as the guys came in for their gloves. "Now hold them."

The Tornadoes knocked in a run in the first and another one in the second. The Thunderballs crept ahead by one in the top of the third, but the Tornadoes picked up two to go into the lead 4 to 3.

"Hey, Nick!" shouted Bugs Wheeler.

"When are you guys going to buy your coach a uniform?"

"When you buy a muzzle for your mouth!" Nick yelled back. He wasn't going to let Bugs get away with every remark he made.

"That's telling him, Nick!" a Thunderball fan shouted.

Frankie Morrow, batting for Johnny Linn in the fourth, poled a long homer. Bill Dakes flied out. Then Gale, batting for Jerry, singled. And Nick, going in for Jim, drove a streaking grounder over the third-base sack for a double. The coach held Gale up at third. Scotty, pinch-hitting for Tom, flied out to deep short.

"Settle down, Lefty!" shouted a Tornadoes fan. "Smoke those pitches in there so they can't see 'em!"

He didn't smoke one past Mike Todey.

100

Mike singled through second, driving in both Gale and Nick. Then Wayne flied out for the second time. Three away.

The Tornadoes' bench was extremely quiet. Mr. Stevens looked concerned, and Bugs Wheeler seemed to have already purchased a muzzle and was wearing it. Nick grinned. Wouldn't it be something to beat the Tornadoes again? Then Mr. Stevens would think twice before considering the Thunderballs a pushover, and Bugs Wheeler's mouth would be muzzled for good.

The Tornadoes tied it up during their turn at bat, giving them, especially Bugs, an opportunity to blow their horns again. In the top of the fifth the Thunderballs failed to score. The Tornadoes came up and knocked in two to go into the lead 8 to 6.

"Come on, Nick!" the guys shouted as Nick stepped to the plate to lead off the last inning. "Start it off with a long blast!"

"You don't really think you'll do that, do you, Nick?" needled Bugs, smiling behind his face mask.

"Watch me," answered Nick.

Nick followed Lefty's first pitch carefully. Too low. The next one looked good. He swung. A long, clean, solid drive to deep left! The fans started to shout and whistle . . . even before the ball sailed over the fence!

"Were you watching?" Nick said to Bugs as he crossed the plate.

"Just lucky," Bugs mumbled.

"One more run ties it up!" Mom said excitedly. "Let's go after it, Scotty!"

Scotty tried. He singled. Mike flied out. Then Wayne singled, advancing Scotty to

second. That's where he stayed. Cyclone fanned and Pat popped up, ending the ball game. The Tornadoes won 8 to 7.

Outside of the Tornadoes' dugout Coach Stevens's face was beaming again. "Good game, Coach!" he yelled. "Gave us quite a battle!"

"Glad you thought so!" replied Mom, with that cool, unruffled smile of hers. You'd think the Thunderballs had won the game instead of the Tornadoes.

"I'd like to know what that secret is between you and Mr. Stevens, Dad," said Nick as they rode home in the car.

Dad grinned. "Sorry. A secret's a secret," he said.

Two days later the Thunderballs redeemed themselves by beating the Clowns.

Wayne and Scotty came over at eight

o'clock that evening and played with Nick's chess set in the tent. Wayne's family had returned from their cottage two days ago and Wayne seemed glad to be back. Guess he would rather be with a lot of friends than spend a vacation at a lake cottage with a boat, a surfboard, and probably all the ice cream and soda he could eat and drink.

Scotty easily beat Wayne the first game and also won the second, though not as easily. Nick, watching them play, was amused at how cautiously Wayne maneuvered his pawns and bishops. Chess was a game that took a lot of concentration and patience. Wayne was using both. In the third game Scotty still had several pawns left on the board when Wayne said, "Checkmate!"

Sure enough, he had Scotty blocked

from all directions. Then he challenged Nick. Nick beat him a game. By now it was getting dark and time for Wayne to go home.

"How about playing tomorrow?" Wayne asked.

"Sure. Come over in the afternoon. You've caught on pretty fast, Wayne. And you never played chess before?"

Wayne shook his head. "Never. It's a great game. I like it."

Wayne and Scotty went home and Nick went into the house. Mom was at the telephone. She seemed extremely concerned about something. Presently she hung up the receiver.

"What's the matter, Mom?" asked Jen. "What did Mrs. Maylor want?"

"She called to remind me that I'm in charge of the program at the Women's

Club at church on Tuesday night," said Mom, frowning thoughtfully. "It was planned so long ago that I had forgotten about it."

Nick went to the bulletin board where Mom tacked notes and looked at the baseball schedule. Next Tuesday the Thunderballs were playing the Knicks.

He turned to Mom, his face pale. "You didn't say you'd do it, did you, Mom? We're playing the Knicks on Tuesday."

She nodded. "I said yes, Nick. It's too late to back out now. It wouldn't be fair to make them find someone else at this late date."

He crumpled into a chair. Guess Mom was right. But you might as well consider that game lost even before it started.

13

DAD took over the coaching job on Tuesday against the Knicks. He quit work early purposely so he could. Johnny Linn pitched and had bad luck from the very start. He walked the first two men. Then an error by Nick gave the Knicks their first run.

The Knicks stretched their lead to five runs after picking up two in the second and two in the third. Monk Jones, hurling for them, seemed to do everything right. Trailing 5 to 0, the Thunderballs came alive in the top of the fourth and knocked in two runs. Dad's strategy to bunt Monk Jones as much as possible worked sometimes, but most of the Thunderballs weren't able to bunt well enough.

"We want Coach *Mrs.* Vassey!" a fan yelled. "Where's Coach *Mrs.* Vassey?"

Laughter started in the stands and presently the entire crowd had caught the laughter bug.

Nick smiled at Dad, who was taking it in good fun. "Guess they want Mom, Dad."

"So I hear. And I wish she were here. Believe me!"

In the top of the fifth the Knicks' shortstop missed Bill Dakes's skyscraping pop fly. Jerry Wong tripled, scoring Bill. But no one knocked Jerry in, and the score remained 5 to 3. In the bottom of the fifth an error by Gale in center field and an error by Cyclone at third helped the Knicks fill the bases.

"We want Coach *Mrs.* Vassey!" a fan yelled again. "Where's Coach *Mrs.* Vassey?"

"You think she could have kept those guys from making errors?" another fan piped up.

"No! But I think the boys play better for her than they do for her husband!" answered the first fan, and then roared with laughter. A dozen or so other fans burst out laughing, too.

"Mow 'em down, Johnny!" another Thunderball fan shouted. "Smoke that pill by 'em!"

The Knicks' batter watched the first pitch breeze past him for a called strike. He struck at the next one and met it solidly. A two-bagger that cleaned the bases.

The Knicks picked up another run before the Thunderballs managed to get them out. Knicks 9 — Thunderballs 3.

The Thunderballs rallied for two runs in the top of the sixth, but could get no more. The game went to the Knicks.

Mom had hardly entered the house that night when Sue yelled, "The Knicks trimmed the Thunderballs nine to five!"

"Quiet, Sue!" Nick glared at her. "Can't you let Mom get inside first before you give her that news?"

Mom looked at the faces around her. Her gaze finally settled on her husband. "We can't win them all, dear," she said and grinned at him.

Mom relaxed in an easy chair in the living room and told them about her program at the club. Nick and the girls filled her in on some of the things that had happened in the ball game. Dad seemed to have very little to add.

At nine-thirty the phone rang in the dining room. Jen set aside the book she was reading to answer it. "For you, Mom," she said.

"It's probably Mrs. Maylor," muttered Nick. "She probably wants Mom to run another program."

Nick tried to strain his ears to hear Mom's side of the conversation, but he couldn't. After a while Mom was back in the living room.

Mom looked at Nick. She was frowning. "That was Mrs. Snow," she said. "She and Mr. Snow just got home from seeing a play and Wayne isn't home. They had left the door open for him and he's been home. His uniform's there. But he is nowhere around and they're worried."

14

"I HAVEN'T seen him since the ball game," said Nick. "I don't know where he could've gone. He doesn't seem to have any other friends he visits."

"Even if he does, he should have gone home by now," said Dad.

"I'll call up Scotty and a couple of other guys," said Nick. "Maybe one of them has seen him."

He made the calls. Scotty said no, he didn't know where Wayne was. "How about me calling a couple guys and you calling a couple guys?" he suggested. "Then I'll call you back?"

"Good idea," replied Nick and they decided who to call. Neither of the guys Nick called knew where Wayne was. When Scotty called his news wasn't good either.

"Okay, thanks, Scotty."

"No luck," Nick said to Mom.

Dad looked at his wristwatch. "The Snows could call the local radio station and have them make an announcement that Wayne is missing."

"But the station's off the air," reminded Mom. "They sign off at eight o'clock."

"How about calling the police?" suggested Nick.

"No," said Dad. "That would be up to the Snows." He shook his head. "Wayne's never disappeared like this before, has he?"

"Not that I know of," said Nick. "I can't understand it."

115

And then a thought struck him. Chess. The tent. "That's a beauty," Wayne had said the first time he had seen it. "Ever spend a night in it?"

"Oh, sure," Nick remembered saying.

It was just possible . . . Without thinking further he put on a light jacket, got a flashlight and headed for the door.

"Nick, where are you going?" Dad asked.

"To the tent," answered Nick. "I'll be right back."

He closed the door softly behind him, then stole up to the tent, flashing the light ahead of him. He drew the flaps apart and looked inside. In the silence he heard soft

breathing. He turned the light toward the cot and caught his breath. There was Wayne Snow, stretched out under a blanket, fast asleep!

Nick went in and shook him. "Wayne! Get up!"

Wayne jerked awake. Nick turned the flashlight away so that the light wouldn't blind him. "I must've fallen asleep," murmured Wayne.

"I guess you did," replied Nick. "Your folks are looking for you."

Wayne flung the blanket aside and followed Nick out of the tent. There was a sound on the porch and Nick saw Mom and Dad standing there.

"He's here," said Nick. "He was sleeping in the tent."

"Gracious!" cried Mom, and clattered down the steps in her slippers. "You've given a lot of people quite a scare, Wayne. Why did you do a thing like that and not say anything?"

"I didn't mean to fall asleep. I just wanted to be here awhile, is all."

"Your mother and father are dreadfully worried about you."

"Yeah, I bet."

Mom frowned. "What?"

"Nothing."

Mom and Dad looked at each other. Then Mom put an arm around Wayne's shoulders. "Come on. I'll drive you home."

"Good night, Wayne," said Nick.

"Good night, Nick," Wayne answered.

15

ON Friday, August 5, the Thunder-balls played the Zebras. The sky was cloudy and getting darker every minute. A storm was brewing in the west.

The teams played four innings before the rain came and halted everything. Fans scattered out of the park to their cars or whatever shelter they could find. The Thunderballs and the Zebras sought the shelter of their dugouts.

After a while the base and plate umpires got together, discussed the situation and called off the game. Since it had gone at least four innings, the Thunderballs, leading 7 to 3, were declared the winners.

On August 11 they played the Tornadoes for the third time, not counting the practice game. It was the Tornadoes' last game of the season. Tomorrow's game between the Thunderballs and the Clowns would be the last for the Thunderballs.

The Tornadoes had beaten the Zebras on Wednesday, leaving them with a record of six wins and five losses. Up till today the Thunderballs' record was seven wins and three losses. If they beat the Tornadoes today they would clinch the pennant.

If! A small word, thought Nick. But it meant so much!

From the Tornadoes' dugout Coach Stevens was watching his star hurler, Lefty Burns, warming up. Now and then he glanced toward the Thunderballs' bench. Could it be that he was worried?

Nick grinned and looked at Mom. She was in the dugout, writing up the batting order. It was hard to tell whether she was nervous.

After a while the Tornadoes infielders took their practice and then the Thunderballs took theirs. A few minutes later the ball game began.

The crowd was the largest Nick had seen at the park. He stood by the dugout and watched, hoping to see the Snows. But in the sea of faces it was almost impossible to recognize anyone.

Frankie Morrow, on the mound for the Thunderballs, took his time. The infielders were giving him all the verbal support they could. "Down the groove, Frankie!"

"Breeze it by 'im, Frankie!"

"The old go, kid! Let's get 'em outa there!"

Frankie toed the rubber, stretched, delivered. A bunt down the third-base line! Pat seemed to be taken by surprise; he started after the ball too late. By the time he got it and pegged to first, the runner was there. The Tornado was given a hit.

"Let's wake up, boys!" shouted Mom, sitting beside Nick in the dugout. "Keep on your toes!"

Nick looked toward the Tornadoes' dugout. Just as he thought . . . nearly the entire Tornadoes' bench was laughing.

"You tell 'em, Coach!" Bugs Wheeler yelled. "They'll need it!"

Another bunt! And again toward third! Pat, playing in, fielded it. He started to throw to second, saw that he might not get the runner, then pegged to first. Out!

The next hitter drove a hard grounder to short. Jim fielded it, pegged to first. Two outs!

The next hitter tagged a long one to left center that went for a double, scoring the runner. Frankie struck the next man out.

Jerry Wong was the only one who managed to get a hit in the bottom of the inning. He died on second. The Tornadoes picked up another run when they came to bat.

"A run an inning!" yelled Bugs Wheeler. "That's enough to beat the Thunderballs!"

"Can't someone knock a foul ball right square into his big mouth?" muttered Scotty.

Mom laughed. "Let him enjoy himself, Scotty. Our laugh will come. Remember, 'He who laughs last . . .'"

"'Laughs best,'" finished Scotty.

"Or 'longest.'"

Wayne led off. He took a called strike, then two balls. Then he leaned into a low pitch and drove it solidly toward deep left field. It kept going . . . going . . . going . . . A home run!

The smile on Wayne's face as he crossed the plate was the first real one Nick had seen in a long time. The guys gripped his hand. The fans cheered and clapped.

"Okay. The ice is broken," Mom said. "Let's keep it cracking."

Russ hit a high one that pierced the sky then came down only to be caught by the second baseman. Pat beat out a slow grounder to short, bringing up Frankie who got a loud hand from the fans. Frankie fouled two pitches, then fanned for out number two. Bill laced a double over the second baseman's head, scoring Pat. Then Jerry flied out. The score was tied at 2 all.

The Tornadoes' lead-off man tried to

bunt the first pitch and missed. He took a ball, then hit a hard grounder back at Frankie. Frankie tossed the ball to first for an easy out. The next batter hit a high foul ball over Wayne's head. Wayne caught it. A hit and an error put two men on, but Frankie struck out the next man for the third out.

"What happened to that run an inning, Bugsy?" Nick yelled across to the Tornado catcher.

Bugs smiled. "Don't worry! We'll pick it up the next time!"

Jim led off in the bottom of the third. A Texas leaguer over short! Then Tom Warren laid into Lefty Burns's first pitch and drilled it to right center, scoring Jim. Nick, in the coaching box at third, held Tom up at the third-base sack. Mike struck out.

"Another blast, Wayne!" the fans shouted as Wayne came to bat.

He blasted one, a high fly to center field. The fielder stepped back three steps and pulled it in. Tom tagged up, then ran in to score. Russ flied out for the second time. Three away. But they had gone ahead by two runs.

"Okay, Nick," said Mom. "Take short in place of Jim. Gale, take center field. Scotty, left field. Cyclone, third base. And *hold* them."

16

COACH Stevens was standing outside of the dugout, his voice booming above those of the crowd. "Come on, Tommy! You're better than he is! Get on, boy!"

Tommy got on.

Mom shouted to Cyclone at third base to play in on the grass in case of a bunt. But the next hitter didn't bunt. He laced a pitch between third and short for a single, advancing the runner to second. The third hitter socked a hard grounder to Nick. Nick fumbled it, then retrieved it in time to throw out the man at third. One away. Men on first and second.

Frankie rubbed the ball, then lifted off his cap and wiped his forehead with the sleeve of his jersey. It was a scorching hot day. Clouds lay like tattered strings across the sky. Many of the fans wore dark glasses. Those who didn't squinted against the sunlight.

Frankie toed the rubber, nodded at the signal from Wayne, then stretched and delivered. The ball breezed in belt-high and the batter swung. The blow was solid. The ball sailed over second, heading for the vacant space between right and center fields. It was good for three bases. The Tornadoes couldn't knock the man in but they had evened the score, 4 to 4.

Nick didn't want to look toward the Tornadoes' bench, but he couldn't help it.

Bugs Wheeler had just said something to Coach Stevens and was laughing as if it were very funny.

The Thunderballs banged out two hits against Lefty during their turn at bat, but could not score. The Tornadoes came to bat in the top of the fifth and started to hit Frankie all over the lot.

Nick looked at Mom. What was she waiting for? The Tornadoes to get 16 runs off him?

"Mom!" he shouted and turned red as he realized that he must have been heard all over the diamond. Laughter rippled from the fans.

A run scored. A man walked. Another one hit.

"For crying out loud, Mom!" This time he hardly cared.

"Nick! Stop yelling at her like that! She knows what she's doing!"

The strong voice came from behind him. Nick turned and looked at Gale Matson.

"Yell all you want, Nick," said Gale. "But not at your mom. You'll just shake her up. Leave her alone."

The words sank into Nick and bit a little, made him think. Gale was right. He had no business yelling at Mom like that. And how many kids' mothers would have the courage to take on a coaching job? Nick realized that he was quite proud of Mom.

The Tornadoes scored another run, and then Mom took Frankie out and put in Johnny Linn. There were two on and one away. A tough spot for Johnny.

He pitched to the first hitter and struck him out amid loud cheers from the fans. "One more, Johnny!" his teammates yelled. "One more!"

A line drive over short! A run scored!

The next man flied out, ending the half-inning. Tornadoes 7 — Thunderballs 4.

"What I hate to see worst of all is the Tornadoes' winning the pennant again this year," snorted Scotty as he sat down.

"Don't give up hope," advised Mom confidently. "Even if we lose today we can still win the pennant by winning tomorrow. Pick up a bat and hustle to the plate, Scotty. You're first hitter."

"Start it off, Scotty," said Nick. "I'd like to bat this inning."

Scotty waited out the pitches, then smashed a single through second base. Mike glanced over his shoulder at Mom, then strode to the plate. Mom must have given him the bunt sign because he laid the first pitch down the third-base line for a perfect bunt. The third baseman was caught flat-footed, but the pitcher fielded the ball and threw Mike out.

Nick stared at Mom. "Aren't we too far behind to bunt?" he asked. She couldn't have used her noodle on that play. Teams usually did not bunt when they were three runs behind and there was only one more inning to go.

Mom tapped his knee gently. "Do we have to do the expected all the time?" she said. "Mike hasn't been hitting. He's popped up and struck out his first two times up. I was hoping he could have fooled the Tornadoes enough to get on, too."

Gale, sitting at Nick's other side, shoved his knee against Nick's. "What did I tell you? She knows what she's doing. Just leave her alone."

Mom laughed. "Why thanks, Gale!" she said.

Wayne, his shoulders wet from perspiration, stepped to the plate. He had hom-

ered the first time up and had socked a sacrifice fly the second time. He took a called strike, a ball, another ball, then swung. A grass-cutting grounder through the mound that just missed Lefty's legs! The hit went for two bases, scoring Scotty.

Russ smashed a single over the second baseman's head, and the Thunderball fans stood up and cheered as Wayne scored.

"One more run and it's tied up! Keep the rally going!" shouted Mom.

Cyclone, who had flied out in the fourth inning, flied out again. He seemed so disappointed he shook his head all the way back to the dugout.

"Cheer up, Cyclone," said Nick. "You'll have another chance next inning."

Johnny walked and the head of the lineup was up again — Bill Dakes. He belted a hit over the third-base sack. Russ scored from second. The coach halted Johnny at third. Again the fans went wild. The game was tied up!

"A hit, Gale!" they shouted. "A hit!"

But Gale Matson flied out.

"Just hold them," pleaded Mom. "Just *hold* them!"

The Thunderballs held the Tornadoes. One out. Two outs. And then the Tornadoes began to hit. A double. A single. And then a triple — before the Thunderballs could get them out.

"The game isn't over yet," said Mom. "Nick, get on."

Nick led off. Two runs behind, he thought. They needed three to win. Possible, but not probable.

The pitch. He swung. A long, long drive! The ball was reaching for the sky in left field! The crowd was screaming. And then the ball disappeared . . . over the fence!

"The old powerhouse, himself," smiled Gale as Nick came running in. "Too bad there weren't men on."

Scotty flied out to left. Mike doubled, Wayne walked. But that was it. Russ fanned and Cyclone flied out again. The Tornadoes took the game 9 to 8.

Now the Tornadoes had a chance at the pennant. They had seven wins and five losses and the Thunderballs had seven wins, four losses with one more game to play. Nick realized that if they lost to the Clowns on Friday, the Thunderballs and Tornadoes would be tied at six and six and would tangle again in a play-off.

17

"A REAL good game, Coach," Coach Stevens said to Mom, with that broad, amused smile of his. Nick watched them shake hands.

"At least we gave the fans their money's worth, didn't we?" Mom said. Her eyes were sparkling but Nick could tell she wasn't as happy as she looked. It would have been great to have knocked off the Tornadoes.

"You still have tomorrow's game to play," said Coach Stevens. "Naturally I can't wish you luck in it."

"Naturally," Mom echoed. "For if we win, we also win the pennant. And you wouldn't want *me* — a woman who's coaching for the first time in her life — to do *that,* would you?"

Coach Stevens chuckled. "Well, I'm looking forward to that play-off."

Dad came up beside them. "All I can say, Coach Vassey, is that you win that game tomorrow, or else."

Mom beamed up at him. "And all I can say, Mr. Vassey, is let's wait and see."

It seemed that all the parents of both teams were attending the Clowns-Thunderballs game the next day, Friday, plus most of the people of Flat Rock. Gale Matson's parents were there. So were Wayne Snow's. Nick looked twice at the Snows to see if he was right. Yes, they were the Snows, all right. Mr. and Mrs. Snow and

Ron. They were sitting halfway up the stands behind the third-base dugout, the dugout which today belonged to the Thunderballs.

The Clowns, batting first, could do nothing against Johnny Linn that first inning. A walk, a flyout, and then two singles in succession gave the Thunderballs a one-run lead. Nick, sitting it out until Mom put him in, watched Stinky Morrison carefully. Stinky, the Clowns' left-handed pitcher, had always worried Nick. He wished the Thunderballs would pile up a heap of runs before he went in.

The Clowns picked up two in the top of the second as a result of two errors, one by Jim at short and another by first baseman Russ Gray.

"I hope they get *that* out of their system right now," Mom said.

The Thunderballs scored a zero at their turn at bat. So did the Clowns in the top of the third. Then, in the bottom of the third, the Thunderballs cut loose. Jerry Wong started it with a double. Jim and Tom both got out. But Mike tagged a high pitch for two bases, scoring Jerry. And Wayne blasted a long triple to the left-field fence, scoring Mike.

Nick, coaching at third, looked behind him and saw the Snows clapping and cheering like teen-agers. Wayne, at third, looked as sober-faced as if hitting triples were something he did all the time. Russ knocked him in, Pat flied out and that was the end of the third inning.

The Clowns came back strong as ever. Nick, playing shortstop now, muffed a hot grounder that bounded off at a crazy angle and permitted the hitter to get two bases.

Then a home run got the Clowns' fans yelling like a bunch of hyenas.

"Hey, Nick!" Jabber Kane shouted from the third-base coaching box. "Who's going to coach the Thunderballs next year? Your aunt?"

"This game isn't over yet, Jabber!" Nick shouted back.

They scored another run before the Thunderballs could stop them. Clowns 5 — Thunderballs 4.

Johnny led off with a double in the bottom of the fourth. Cyclone, pinch-hitting for Bill, rapped out a single. Pat, now coaching at third, windmilled Johnny home. Then Jerry hit into a double play and Nick struck out.

In the fifth the Clowns roared again. This time Gale fumbled a fly ball in left field, letting in a run. It drew a disappointed moan from the crowd, but a sadder one from Gale. Nick could hear him from short. The Clowns scored twice more to advance into the lead 8 to 5.

"Hey, you Thunderballs!" cried a voice from the stands. "Why don't you throw in your gloves and quit now before you get slaughtered?"

Nick and several other guys looked up. Sure enough it was Bugs Wheeler and five or six other players from the Tornadoes. Not far from them sat Coach Burt Stevens, grinning triumphantly. They clearly had come with hopes of seeing the Clowns whip the Thunderballs. Then the Tornadoes and Thunderballs would be tied for the pennant.

It looked as if their hopes were going to come true. Stinky held the Thunderballs to a double in the bottom of the fifth, and no runs.

The Clowns started off well again as

143

they came up for the sixth and final inning. Cyclone let a grounder zip through his legs. That was it, though. The Clowns couldn't score.

"One, two, three, Stinky!" yelled Bugs Wheeler.

"Dog!" snorted Nick.

Pat, leading off, flied out. Johnny walked. Cyclone flied out. One more out and the ball game would be over.

Then Jerry singled. They were still alive! "Keep it going, Nick!" Mom shouted.

"Save me a rap, Nick!" Gale Matson pleaded.

Nick looked nervously at Stinky. For some unknown reason he was never able to hit Stinky's pitches. He was sure that if he swung away he'd strike out, just as he had done the last time. And that would be it. The ball game would be over, and Bugs

Wheeler, Coach Stevens and the rest of the Tornadoes would never let him live it down. They'd be gloating at the play-off game.

Suddenly he remembered what Mom had said in another game: *Do we have to do the expected all the time?* He looked toward first and then third. The Clowns were playing deep. He could try a bunt. It just might work. What could he lose?

The pitch came in. He shifted his feet and bunted the ball down the third-base line, catching the Clowns completely off their guard! The bunt was perfect!

"Nice going, Nick!" shouted Mom.

Three on and Gale came up. The fans yelled. Gale's parents sat still, waiting patiently.

"There you are, Gale!" yelled Nick. "I saved you a rap! Now, clonk it!"

Stinky stretched and pitched. Gale

swung. *Crack!* A solid smash! A high long ball to deep left! It kept going . . . going . . . Gone over the fence! A home run!

It was over. The Thunderballs — and Mom — had won the pennant.

Gale beamed proudly as he gripped Nick's hand. "Thanks for saving me that rap!"

The Snows came forward and shook hands with Mom. "Wayne thinks an awful lot of you, Mrs. Vassey," said Mrs. Snow. "He's always talking about you and your family. I wonder if you all would come over some day soon. My husband and I would love to have you. Will you?"

Mom's face shone radiantly. "We'll be glad to, Mrs. Snow."

Another figure joined the small group. Burt Stevens. A smile was on his face but it wasn't as broad as it had been. He stretched out his hand to shake Mom's.

"Congratulations, Coach," he said. "You won it fair and square."

Mom's eyes sparkled. "Thank you, Mr. Stevens," she said, and then added mischievously, "Sorry you don't get a chance for a play-off."

"And I won the bet," Dad said. "The Stevenses are taking the Vasseys out for a Chinese dinner. That's the bet we had agreed on in Mr. Wong's restaurant. Tomorrow okay, Coach Stevens?"

"Tomorrow's fine," smiled Mr. Stevens.

How many of these Matt Christopher sports classics have you read?

Baseball

❑ Baseball Pals
❑ Catcher with a Glass Arm
❑ Challenge at Second Base
❑ The Diamond Champs
❑ The Fox Steals Home
❑ Hard Drive to Short
❑ The Kid Who Only
    Hit Homers
❑ Little Lefty
❑ Long Stretch at First Base
❑ Look Who's Playing
    First Base
❑ Miracle at the Plate
❑ No Arm in Left Field
❑ Shortstop from Tokyo
❑ The Submarine Pitch
❑ Too Hot to Handle
❑ The Year Mom Won
    the Pennant

Basketball

❑ The Basket Counts
❑ Johnny Long Legs
❑ Long Shot for Paul
❑ Red-Hot Hightops

Dirt Bike Racing

❑ Dirt Bike Racer
❑ Dirt Bike Runaway

Football

❑ Catch That Pass!
❑ The Counterfeit Tackle
❑ Football Fugitive
❑ The Great Quarterback
    Switch
❑ Tight End
❑ Touchdown for Tommy
❑ Tough to Tackle

Ice Hockey

❑ Face-Off
❑ The Hockey Machine
❑ Ice Magic

Soccer

❑ Soccer Halfback

Track

❑ Run, Billy, Run

All available in paperback from Little, Brown and Company

Join the Matt Christopher Fan Club!

To become an official member of the Matt Christopher Fan Club,
send a self-addressed, stamped envelope (10 x 13, 3 oz. of postage) to:

Matt Christopher Fan Club
34 Beacon Street
Boston, MA 02108

No Arm in Left Field

NO ARM
IN LEFT FIELD

by Matt Christopher

Illustrated by Byron Goto

Little, Brown and Company

BOSTON TORONTO LONDON

Library of Congress Cataloging-in-Publication Data
Christopher, Matthew F
    No arm in left field.

    [1. Baseball—Stories] I. Goto, Byron, illus.
II. Title.
PZ7.C458No   [Fic]   73-12296
ISBN 0-316-13964-5
ISBN 0-316-13990-4 (pbk.)

HC: 10   9   8   7   6   5   4
PB: 10   9   8

                        VB

Published simultaneously in Canada
by Little, Brown & Company (Canada) Limited

Printed in the United States of America

to Kenny VanSickle

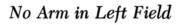

No Arm in Left Field

1

TERRY DELANEY took a couple of steps closer to Mick Jordan to make sure his throw wouldn't fall short, and winged the ball. The worn, dirt-stained sphere arced through the air and landed in Mick's outstretched glove. A short throw didn't bother him, but he just didn't have the arm for throwing a long distance.

"Who'd you play with on Long Island?" Mick asked, pushing his long black hair out of his eyes.

"The Fall City Tigers." Terry smiled.

"Know where we finished up? Next to last!"

Mick laughed. Terry had been telling him about the small town on Long Island where he had lived before moving to Forest Lake, a suburb in eastern Pennsylvania. Terry's father, an engineer, had taken a job with a mining concern and brought his family here in the middle of the winter. Within weeks Mrs. Delaney had joined the Great Books Club in Forest Lake, and Connie, Terry's fifteen-year-old sister, had become a varsity cheerleader. The family settled easily into the life of their new town.

Terry, himself a junior high student, had liked winter sports but was pleased that at last summer had finally rolled around, for with it had come his favorite sport, baseball.

"You have a league here?" he asked.

"Of course," said Mick, reaching forward to grab Terry's soft throw. "I play with the Forest Lakers. We're having practice in a little while. Want to come with me?"

Terry's eyes brightened. "You don't have to ask me twice!" he replied happily.

Just then a voice shouted from across the street. "Hey, Mick!"

Mick held up his throw, turned, and looked at the kid who had yelled. Terry looked, too. A tall, dark-haired boy wearing a knit sweater and bell-bottom pants came running across the street. He stopped on the sidewalk, let his gaze linger a while on Terry, then motioned to Mick.

"Come here, will ya?" he said.

His voice was commanding. Terry felt

5

a sudden change in the atmosphere, as if it had become charged with electricity.

Mick tossed the ball to Terry. "Just a second, Terry," he said, and trotted over to the newcomer.

"Who's the Negro kid?" Terry heard the newcomer ask plainly.

Terry's face grew hot, but his eyes narrowed and he stared at the boy. He didn't hear Mick's response, nor could he hear anymore of what the newcomer said. He had a good idea of the gist of it, however, and that was enough. He shook his head and looked away.

After a minute Mick's voice was loud enough for Terry to hear. "Come on. He's okay, I tell you."

Terry looked at them, and noticed that the newcomer had a baseball glove and was wearing sneakers.

Terry turned and started for his house, tossing the baseball into the air and catching it as it came down. He wasn't going to wait around all day. He whistled in order to drown out the voices behind him.

It had happened again, he thought, his stomach churning. *A white kid who doesn't like a black kid. But I bet that one of his favorite baseball players, or football players, is black.*

"Hey, Terry! Wait a minute!"

He paused without turning around, and heard Mick's footsteps pounding up behind him.

"Terry." Mick stopped before him, breathing hard. "Terry, I'm sorry."

Terry smiled. "Oh, that's okay. I've seen his kind before. He on your team?"

"He's our shortstop."

"Is he good?"

"Yes, he is."

Terry looked over his shoulder, saw the kid begin to walk briskly away and then pause near a bush to look back.

"He's waiting for you," Terry said. "Better get going."

"Aren't you coming?" Mick asked.

"No." Terry flashed a grin. "Go on, Mick. Don't worry about me. I'll be all right."

Mick shook his head. "I don't know what to say, Terry. I wanted him to meet you. I was surprised when he said he — he didn't want to." He wiped his forehead with the back of his hand. "I feel funny, Terry."

Terry chuckled. "I know. That's because it's brand new to you. Not to me, though I'll never get used to it. Go ahead,

he's waiting. I've got things to do, anyway." He turned and headed for the porch.

"See you later, Terry," Mick said.

"Sure, Mick."

Terry opened the screen door and stepped onto the porch. He closed it and saw Mick running across the lawn toward the kid who was waiting for him. He wasn't sure, but he thought he saw the kid smile.

Connie met him as he stepped into the house. Even though she was three years older she was only an inch taller than her athletic brother.

"Who's the kid with Mick?" she asked.

"I don't know. Mick didn't tell me and I didn't ask him."

"Where are they going?"

"To the ball field. Their team's practic-ing."

He started past her and she grabbed his arm. Her eyes were hard as she looked at him. "I know you want to play, Terry. Why didn't you go with Mick?"

He reached over and gently lifted her hand from his arm. "Because I'm black, my dear sister, and that other kid just don't like black." A smile cracked his face. "You've heard of *that* before, haven't you?"

Connie didn't flinch. "Maybe that kid's the only one who feels that way. There are other black families in this town."

"I know. But that kid is sure to have friends, and his friends are likely to go along with him. You should've heard him. 'Who's the "Negro" kid?' he asked Mick in

11

that tone they use and loud enough so I can hear. Right away I pegged him. He's a leader, Connie. He's the type guys follow."

"You're just guessing, Terry. You don't know for sure."

"Okay, I don't know for sure. But I'll bet on it."

The sun was dropping toward the western horizon when a knock sounded on the door. Mrs. Delaney answered it.

"Terry, it's Mick," she said.

Terry left the TV set where he had been watching a sports program and met Mick at the door. Mick's hair was tousled and his face shiny with sweat.

"Hi, Terry," he greeted him. "Got some news for you. We need an outfielder."

Terry crossed his arms. "Don't look at me," he said.

"But you said that you'd like to play!" Mick exclaimed. "And there's nobody else. Come on, Terry. Please come to our next practice. I've told Coach Harper about you."

Soft footsteps sounded behind Terry and he looked over his shoulder. The warm, pleasant face of his father grinned at him.

"Hi, Mick," Mr. Delaney said. "I heard what you said to Terry. I think it's a good idea."

"What about that kid who was here earlier?"

"Tony Casterline? He can lump it for all I care!"

Terry laughed. Still, he wasn't sure he

13

wanted to join a team on which even one member had a grudge against a black boy's playing. And, as he had said to Connie, there could be others.

He finally agreed, however, when Dad, Mom and Connie put in their nickel's worth. He would give it a try, at least. Who knew but what his playing — if he could only perform well — might make Tony Casterline forget his prejudice and turn him into a friend? Such things happened. If only his arm were stronger . . .

The next afternoon Mick stopped at the house. Together they walked to the ballfield where Terry was introduced to Coach Don Harper and the members of the Forest Lakers baseball team. Some nodded their greeting, some shook hands. Tony Casterline was one of the former.

Terry couldn't help but feel conspicuous. He was the only black boy in the group. He noticed, though, that there was another boy whose skin was darker than the others, whose features suggested a nationality from, he guessed, a country in South America. The boy's name was Caesar Valquez.

Terry wondered briefly how Caesar was accepted when he had first come to Forest Lake. Or was he born here?

"Okay, guys," Coach Harper said, carrying a bat and ball to the plate. "Outfielders, hustle out there. Terry, get out in left. Infielders, play catch."

Coach Harper's hits to the outfielders ranged from line drives to sky-reaching blows. Terry didn't have a miss and welcomed the coach's praises of "Nice going,

15

Terry!" and "Hey, we've got an out-fielder!"

Batting practice turned into a lot of fun, too. The team batted twice around and Terry knocked his share of grounders and long flies to his usual corner, deep left. His bunting, though, suffered.

"We're having a practice game with the Boilers tomorrow afternoon," the coach said to Terry when practice was over. "Like to have you here."

Terry smiled. "I'll be here," he promised.

He almost forgot Tony Casterline's coldness as he walked home with Mick. All he could think about was telling Mom, Dad and Connie that the coach liked his playing and wanted him at the practice game tomorrow.

Then he remembered something else,

and he turned to his friend. "Thanks, Mick," he said. "If it weren't for you, I wouldn't be playing baseball."

Mick's eyes glimmered. "Aw, forget it, Terry," he said. "Somebody would've asked you to play."

A hot June sun blazed down on the baseball field the next afternoon. The teams tossed a coin to see who would bat last, and the Boilers won. Pitching for them was a red-headed left-hander, Lefty Wallace.

The first three batters for the Forest Lakers were Jeff Roberts, Tony Casterline and Terry Delaney. Terry couldn't believe it. Third batter!

Lefty's speed worked like magic. Both Jeff and Tony popped up to the infield. After fouling two pitches Terry struck out on a high, outside throw.

"That was over your head, man!" Tony cried.

Terry ignored him as he dropped the bat, got his glove, and ran out to his position.

The first pitch Mick Jordan delivered to the Boilers' lead-off man was hit through the hole between first and second base. The man held up at first as right fielder Caesar Valquez fielded the ball and pegged it to second.

The second batter failed on two bunt attempts, then drilled a long fly to deep left. Terry backpedaled for it, caught it, then whipped it to third base. The ball barely reached the halfway point between him and the infield. The runner on first — after tagging up — ran to second, then bolted to third.

Third baseman Ed Caliel rushed out

19

to receive the throw in, but the runner was safely on base by the time he got it and turned to throw.

"Hold it!" Mick yelled.

A second voice sliced through the air, and Terry's ears filled with its terrible ring.

"Hey! See that? Terry hasn't got an arm! He can't throw worth beans!"

2

TERRY TWINGED. He couldn't rid himself of his poor throwing arm. It was his big weakness.

Once, a couple of years ago, he had played second base, where he didn't have to throw very hard. But his coach had discovered that Terry was better at catching flies than grounders, and so had transferred him to the outfield. Terry liked that better and had played there ever since, even if he did have trouble when a long fly was hit while men were on base.

He saw the angry look on Tony's face,

and heard a chuckle come from center fielder Rich Muldoon.

"Why don't you trade in that arm, Terry?" the tall, skinny kid hollered at him. "You sure can't get a worse one!"

Terry grinned. "I'll make up for it in other ways, Rich!" he yelled back.

With one out, Mick pitched to the next batter. The Boiler smashed a hot, sizzling liner directly at Ed Caliel at third. The runner on third started toward home, then stopped. He slipped as he tried to get back to third, and Ed doubled him up. Three outs.

"Nice play, Ed," Terry said as he trotted up beside the stocky third baseman.

Ed glanced at him, nodded, and looked away.

"Muldoon, Philips, Caliel," Coach Harper announced. "Get on, Rich."

Rich put on his protective helmet, stepped to the plate, took his swings and struck out. Bud Philips hit a high bouncer to the pitcher for the second out and Ed grounded out to short.

Mick held the Boilers hitless. Then, in the top of the third, Stu Henderson drilled Lefty Wallace's second pitch through the pitcher's mound, forcing Lefty to dance a momentary jig. It was the Forest Lakers' first hit of the game and the guys got excited.

Caesar Valquez stepped to the plate, dug his sneakers into the soft dirt as if he were going to wallop one of Lefty's pitches into no man's land, and then stuck the bat out for a bunt.

Foul.

Caesar stepped out of the box, glanced

at the coach and stepped back in again. Another bunt, and again a foul.

"Hit away, Ceez!" Coach Harper yelled.

Caesar blasted the next pitch to center for an easy out. Mick, last man in the batting order, removed the metal doughnut from the fat part of his bat, plodded to the plate, dug his sneakers firmly into the dirt, and watched the first pitch breeze by him.

"Strike!" yelled the ump.

"Clout it, Mick!" Terry cried.

The pitch, and Mick swung. A hot grounder to second base! The Boiler second baseman caught the hop, snapped it to second for the first out, the shortstop whipped it to first. A double play.

The Boiler fans roared as the teams exchanged sides.

Bottom of the third. *Hope nobody*

knocks one too deep in left, Terry thought as he ran out to his position. *I don't want Tony Casterline to be able to embarrass me again.*

A high pop fly to Stu accounted for the first out and Terry breathed a sigh of relief. Then Mick drilled a pitch over the heart of the plate and the Boiler batter drilled it back at him like a rifle shot. It knocked Mick's glove off and bounced out to center for a hit.

Man on first and one out.

Mick toed the rubber and threw. *Crack!* A hefty clout to deep left. Terry turned and bolted back toward the fence, then looked over his shoulder, lifted his glove and snared the ball — a spectacular, one-handed catch. He stopped in his tracks and pegged the ball in to Tony Casterline, throwing it as hard as he could. The ball dropped short, as he expected, and he saw the Boiler runner beeline to second.

"Old no arm!" Tony yelled as he ran out to get the throw in. The runner held up at second.

Terry's heart pounded. Not only from running, but because of Tony's sarcastic remark. Old no arm! That darn guy didn't even give him credit for the catch!

A shot over short scored the Boilers' first run. Terry ran up, caught the ball on a bounce and pegged it successfully to Jeff Roberts at second. The hitter held up on first. Coming in closer to Tony, Terry was able to see a scowl on the shortstop's face.

The Forest Lakers settled down. Stu, crouched behind home plate in his catcher's gear, tried to liven up the team with his peppery chatter. Although this was just a practice game, the guys were serious about every play. Terry wondered how much more serious they could be when league play actually started.

Mick worked the next Boiler batter to two balls and two strikes, then fanned him with a curve.

Jeff, leading off for the Lakers in the top of the fourth, struck out. Tony then laced a pitch through short for a single. Terry came up, hoping to redeem himself for his first strikeout. Lefty threw two inside pitches, then fired one high and outside, which Terry liked.

He swung — and missed. Another high, outside pitch. Again he swung — and missed.

"Two . . . two!" the ump bellowed.

Terry stepped out of the box, rubbed

the bat firmly around its skinny handle, then stepped in again and lambasted Lefty's next pitch to left center field. Tony raced around to third and Terry held up on second for a clean double. Standing on the bag Terry noticed Tony looking at him appraisingly.

The handful of Forest Laker fans cheered Terry, and he felt pleased. He had put himself and Tony in scoring position. Now it was up to the next batters.

Rich Muldoon didn't help. His pop-up to third made it two outs. It was up to Bud Philips. Bud, a lanky, light-haired, left-handed batter, strode to the plate in that lazy fashion of his and watched the first pitch sail by him as if he were watching a parade. He didn't look as if he were going to swing at the next pitch either until after the ball had left Lefty's hand and was halfway to the plate.

Crack! A bullet drive to right center, and both Tony and Terry scored! Ed grounded out to end the rally. Forest Lakers 2, Boilers 1.

The change in the lead seemed to have affected the Boilers. They weren't able to get a man on first base in their half of the inning. In the fifth Stu, Caesar and Mick went down one, two, three. So did the Boilers.

Jeff, leading off for the Lakers in the top of the sixth, singled on the first pitch and scampered to second base on Tony's scratch single. Terry, hoping to knock in at least one run, swung hard at a high, outside one — and missed. He let a low pitch slide by for strike two, then swung

29

hard again at another one he liked — high and outside.

"Strike three!" cried the ump.

"Oh, come on!" Tony yelled angrily. "Somebody knock us in!"

Nobody did.

"This is it!" Coach Harper said as the Lakers ran out to the field. "Let's play heads-up out there!"

Mick worked hard on the Boiler lead-off man and struck him out on the 3–2 pitch. The infielders snapped the ball around the horn, then returned it to Mick.

Mick took his time, then threw one low and inside. Bat met ball and Terry sprinted forward as he saw it heading for short left field. He reached low for the shallow drive and caught the ball near his sneaker laces. He was within ten feet of Tony when he slowed up and tossed the ball to the shortstop.

"Nice catch," Tony said, and smiled crookedly. "Too bad nobody was on second. You might've thrown him out — seeing you didn't have far to throw."

"Guess I was lucky," Terry said as he turned and trotted back to his position. He tried not to get sore. Maybe one of these days — soon, he hoped — Tony would realize that Terry could catch, run and hit well enough to make up for his poor arm, and stop his sarcastic remarks.

Mick walked the next Boiler, the next batter popped out to Ed, and that was it. The Forest Lakers won, 2 to 1.

"Nice game, Terry," Mick said as they stood by the water fountain, waiting for their chance to get a drink.

31

"Thanks, Mick," Terry said, wiping his sweating brow. "You, too."

A couple of strange guys came up and looked at Terry. They were about his age and wore baseball caps.

"Nice hit you got, Delaney," one of them wearing glasses said. "Bet you won't get to first base on us."

A chuckle rippled from him as he nudged his partner and walked away.

"Who are they?" Terry asked curiously.

"Jim Burling and Dave Wilson," said Tony, who was standing nearby. "They're the battery for the Yellow Jackets, the team we play our first league game with. They've got your number, Terry. You're a sucker for high, outside pitches."

3

"FELLAS," Coach Harper said. "Before you leave I've got some nice news for you. There's a movie on the Oakland-Cincinnati World Series tomorrow night at the Forest Lake Hotel, sponsored by the Forest Lake Lions Club, and all of us are invited to attend. How about that?"

A chorus of satisfied shouts resounded from the boys. Terry was especially pleased for the opportunity. He hadn't seen any of the World Series games on television.

Suddenly he remembered that tomorrow night his father had planned to take the family out to dinner. The conflict bothered him. He liked to go out for dinner, but he wanted to see the World Series movie, too.

"Fine," the coach said. "The movie will be shown at seven-thirty. I'll have someone telephone each of you and arrange to pick you up."

"Are you going, Terry?" Mick asked.

"I'd like to," Terry replied. "But we've planned to go out for dinner."

"Skip the dinner," Mick suggested, smiling. "You can't always see a World Series movie."

Terry shrugged. "Okay. I'm sure my dad will take us out for dinner again sometime!"

Terry saw a scornful look come over Tony's face. *Can you beat that?* he thought. *He even resents my going to see a World Series movie with the team!*

Their eyes locked. Then Tony looked away, tapped a couple of his friends on their shoulders, and walked off with them.

"Ready to go?" Terry asked Mick, hoping nobody could hear his pounding heart.

Mick glanced at the three boys leaving. "Let's wait a minute," he said.

"Why? For Tony and those guys to get way ahead of us?" Terry grinned. "If I don't mind them, why should you?"

Mick's eyebrows pulled together above the bridge of his nose. "You mean it doesn't bother you, the way he looked at you and all that"

"I've met guys like Tony before, Mick," Terry said. "I'll always keep meeting guys like him. My father says that'll be something I'll have to live with the rest of my life, and as far as I can see I'm not the one with a problem. Tony is."

"But doesn't it *hurt?*"

"Sure it hurts. But not as much as it used to." He chuckled. "At least, he hasn't called me any dirty names yet — and if he knows what's good for him, he better not."

Mick laughed and socked Terry lightly on the shoulder. "Come on," he said, and they started off the field. "You know, Terry, I can't see why any guy — black or white — can't like you. You know what I'd probably do if I were in your place?"

"What?" Terry asked.

"I'd, well, I'd . . ."

Mick looked at Terry, a vacant expression in his eyes.

"You'd what, Mick?"

Mick inhaled deeply, then breathed out a sigh. "Darn it, Terry, I don't know what I'd do," he admitted.

They walked the rest of the way home in silence, and when Terry told his parents that he wanted to go to the World Series movie instead of to dinner with them, his father didn't blame him.

"We can all have dinner together anytime," he said. "But a World Series movie isn't shown very often."

The next evening the Delaneys left at 6:30, with Terry waiting in the living room for the telephone call. Twice he almost dozed off. The clock on the mantle said 7:00, then 7:15, then 7:30. Still the phone didn't ring.

Had he been forgotten? He tried phoning Mick, but no one answered.

7:45 . . . 8:00 . . .

Suddenly the phone rang. Terry leaped out of the chair and grabbed the receiver. "Yes?" he said excitedly.

"Hello. This is Mrs. Williams of the Great Books Club," said a warm, soothing voice. "Is Mrs. Delaney there?"

Terry's heart sank. "No, she isn't," he answered politely. "Can I take a message?"

"No," the woman said. "I'll call again tomorrow. Thank you."

The phone clicked. Terry hung up and went back to the chair, dejected. He should have gone to the dinner, he thought, instead of sitting here like a bump on a log.

He picked up a magazine and was reading it when his parents and Connie

returned from dinner. They stared sur-
prisedly at him.

"What happened?" his father asked.
"Was the movie canceled?"

"Nobody called," Terry said cheer-
lessly.

"I'm so sorry," Mrs. Delaney said. "I
guess you should have come with us after
all."

He went back to his reading, and was
only half concentrating on the story when
the phone rang again. Quickly he dropped
the magazine and went to answer it.

"Hello?"

"Terry, this is Mick."

"Yes, Mick?"

"Too bad you missed the World Series
movie. It was great!"

Terry's hand froze on the receiver. He

39

stared at the clock on the wall. Ten after nine!

"Nobody called me," he said huskily.

"Didn't Tony call you?"

"*Tony?* Was *he* supposed to call me?"

"Yes! He told me you weren't going. He said that you decided to go to dinner with your family!"

"The liar!" Terry cried. "He never called me at all!"

"The rat," Mick said softly.

Terry saw Tony the next day at practice. He was boiling mad. "Tony, I heard that you were supposed to call me last night," he said, trying to control his rage.

Tony blushed. "I thought you were going to dinner with your family," he said.

"I didn't say I was," Terry shot back. "I said that we had *planned* to go, but

41

that I would go to the World Series movie instead. You must have heard me."

Tony's lips pressed together, then spread apart in a forced smile. "You didn't miss anything," he said. "It wasn't that good."

"I *bet* it wasn't," Terry snapped, and stamped angrily toward the pile of bats. He selected one he liked, slipped a metal doughnut over the fat part of it and began swinging it hard back and forth over his shoulder.

4

LATER, WHILE waiting for supper, Terry and Mick played catch on the front lawn. Terry was trying to strengthen his throwing arm. He *had* to be able to peg the ball to second or third base when it was hit to deep left. Mick had put a handkerchief in his glove to cushion the throws and was catching them with hardly a wince.

"How am I doing?" Terry asked.

"I don't know," Mick answered. "It's hard to tell. Let's go to the ballfield after supper."

43

Mick's father came by and paused on the sidewalk.

"Hi, Mr. Jordan," Terry greeted him. "I'm trying to build up my throwing arm."

"Hi, Dad," Mick said.

"Hi, boys," Mr. Jordan greeted them. He was tall, yellow-haired, and had the long, lithe build of an athlete. "Mind a bit of advice, Terry?"

Terry held up his throw and looked at Mr. Jordan. "Anything you want to tell me is sure welcome, Mr. Jordan," he replied honestly.

Mr. Jordan grinned. "Well, it isn't much, but it might save you a lot of torture later on." He slapped at an annoying bee. "I understand what you're trying to do, but at your age you'd better not throw too hard nor too long or you might come up with a permanent injury in that arm.

44

You're just a kid yet. Your arm isn't strong enough to take it."

"That's why I'm throwing harder," Terry explained, frowning. "So it will be stronger."

"You're taking a chance, Terry," Mr. Jordan warned. "A big chance." He shrugged and started toward home. "Well, don't say I didn't warn you."

Terry smiled. "I won't, Mr. Jordan," he promised, "because, as of right now, I'm going to take your advice."

Terry waited for Mr. Jordan to walk on, then looked at his friend. "Now there's a guy who turns me on, Mick," he said happily. "Not even my own father tells me things like that."

He pegged the ball to Mick, then heard footsteps on the porch behind him.

"That's because your own father doesn't

45

know a thing about baseball," said a voice. Terry turned to see his tall, broad-shouldered father standing behind the screen door, a genial smile on his lips.

Terry chuckled. "Did you hear what Mr. Jordan told me, Dad?"

"I sure did," Mr. Delaney said. "And I think that it makes a lot of sense."

He came off the porch, stopped beside Mick, and began to play catch with the boys.

Presently a dune buggy with a huge flower painted on its hood came buzzing up the street, crept up to the curb, and stopped. Out of it hopped Tony Casterline and Jeff Roberts. Terry saw that the driver looked to be about nineteen or twenty, wore long hair, and had a striking resemblance to Tony.

47

The two boys waved to him as he stepped on the gas and sped away.

Terry looked at Tony and Jeff without speaking. His first impression was that they had come to see him, since the dune buggy had stopped directly in front of his house. But the guys motioned to Mick and ignored him completely.

"Excuse me, Mr. Delaney," Mick said, and ran over to them.

Terry smiled at his father. *Don't worry, Dad*, his look said. *Those guys don't impress me a bit.*

They continued to play catch — just the two of them — and were interrupted when Mrs. Delaney came to the door and told her husband that he had a phone call. He excused himself and went into the house.

48

A minute later Tony and Jeff started to leave, and Mick returned to his post to continue playing catch with Terry.

"Hey, you guys," Terry suddenly called to them. "If you want to join us one of you can use my glove. I've got another one in the house, and one guy can sit out for a while."

Tony and Jeff looked at him, said something to each other, then returned to the lawn. Terry smiled and sent his glove spinning toward the boys.

"You use it," Tony said to Jeff.

Jeff caught it and put it on. As Terry started toward the house for his other glove, Tony called to him, "Never mind, Terry. I don't think your glove is going to feel right to either of us."

Terry looked at him; the real meaning

49

behind Tony's statement hit him like a baseball bat. What Tony meant was that he wouldn't use Terry's glove just because it was Terry's.

Before Terry could decide what to say, Jeff took off the glove and tossed it back to him. "Here," he said. "I really don't think it fits, either."

Terry's face felt hot. He had hoped that his friendly gesture would bear fruit, that it might start to close the gap between them. But his offer had been turned against him in order to humiliate him. His eyes blazed. "All right. If the glove isn't right, let's play bare-handed. That okay with you guys?"

Jeff gazed in sheepish inquiry at Tony. "Yeah, that's okay."

Tony shrugged.

Terry winged the ball to Tony who

gasped at the ball's impact on his hands. "Take it easy, will you, Terry?" Tony asked.

Terry, seeing Tony's discomfort, smiled a bit and nodded agreement. They lobbed the ball between the four of them.

"Your father ever play professional baseball?" Tony asked as he caught a soft throw from Mick.

"No. Just sandlot," Terry replied.

"My father played in the majors," Tony said, a spark of pride in his voice.

"He did? With whom?"

"The Minnesota Twins."

Terry's heart skipped a beat. He had never before met a kid whose father played major league baseball.

"He was an infielder," Tony added.

They tossed the ball back and forth a few more times, and Terry could see that neither Tony nor Jeff were enjoying catching it bare-handed. After awhile Tony said that they had to leave, and they did.

"Aren't you going to ask me what they wanted?" Mick asked.

Terry shrugged. "I figure you'd tell me if you wanted to," he said.

Mick smiled. "They told me that our first league game is Tuesday against the Yellow Jackets. But I already knew that. I think it was just an excuse for them to stop here and cause a bit of trouble."

Terry nodded. "I figured that," he said. "And I'm glad they did. I guess maybe next time they might *want* to use my glove."

Mick chuckled. "I guess they will," he said.

5

THE YELLOW JACKETS had a picture of a fat bee on the front left side of their jerseys. They had first raps and looked extremely confident of winning their first game.

On the mound for the Forest Lakers was Woody Davis, a slim kid with arms like spindles but with plenty of speed. A crowd was divided between a large group in the stands behind the backstop screen and a smattering in the small bleachers behind first and third bases. It was a hot June day and a lot of the women were fanning themselves to keep cool.

The Yellow Jackets' lead-off hitter looked for a walk, and almost got it as Woody worked the count on him to 3–2. Then Woody slid a pitch by him.

"Strike three!" yelled the ump.

In left field Terry Delaney wished that if a ball were hit out to him it would be a shallow drive, one that he wouldn't have trouble throwing in to the infield. The thought had hardly left his mind when *bang!* — a long hit zoomed out to deep left! He ran back . . . back . . . lifted his glove and caught the fly over his head!

The Forest Laker fans cheered as he pegged the ball in. They didn't know, though, how hard his heart was pounding and how relieved he was.

A pop fly to the infield ended the top half of the inning.

Jeff Roberts, leading off for the Forest

Lakers, put on his protective helmet, stepped to the mound, and faced the Yellow Jackets' short, husky pitcher, Jim Durling. Ready to follow him were Tony, Terry, and Rich Muldoon.

Jim released a couple of high pitches, then grooved one down the middle. He grooved the next one too, and Jeff smashed it to center field for a single.

Tony got the signal from Coach Harper to bunt, and laid one down neatly just inside the third-base line. The Yellow Jacket third baseman, waiting for exactly this to happen, nevertheless didn't play in close enough to field the bunt and get Jeff at second. He managed, however, to throw Tony out at first.

Terry let an inside pitch go by for a strike, then swung at a high, outside one that he missed for strike two.

"Bring 'em down, Terry!" yelled Tony, who had run back to the bench.

Terry stepped out of the box and rubbed his hands in the soft dirt, while a chorus of yells rose from the fans. He returned to the box. In came a pitch he liked, and he swung. Foul ball!

Nothing and two. He felt nervous and sweaty. Hundreds of pairs of eyes were focused on him, waiting to see what he would do.

A wide pitch. One and two.

Another pitch looked good to him. He swung hard — and missed. "Strike three!" the ump yelled.

"That was a mile high, Terry!" Tony shouted. "You've got to bring 'em down, man!"

Terry tossed the bat aside and re-

turned, head bowed, to the bench, the roar of the fans lingering in his ears.

"That was high and outside, Terry," Coach Harper said evenly. "Next time step a few inches closer to the plate. See what happens."

Terry nodded.

Rich, the Forest Lakers' cleanup hitter, belted a foul ball into the third-base bleachers, then lambasted a high pitch to deep center. The ball was caught and that was it for the Lakers' half of the inning.

The Yellow Jackets' lead-off hitter cracked Woody's first pitch to right field for a neat single, then made it to second on a sacrifice bunt. First baseman Bud Philips brought the ball to Woody after the put-out, talked to him a minute, then returned to his position.

Woody threw two wide pitches to the

next Yellow Jacket, then grooved one. *Crack!* A blow to deep left center! Both Terry and Rich bolted after it. Terry reached it first, picked it up and heaved it to second base.

The ball hit the ground far short of the bag. Second baseman Jeff Roberts snorted disgustedly as he ran after it. The runner on second scored. And the hitter, after rounding first and second bases, made a beeline for third. Jeff, grabbing up the ball on the outfield grass, pegged it quickly to Ed Caliel. The throw was high and the runner slid safely into the bag.

"A triple!" Tony grunted, casting a burning look at Terry. "A good arm would've got him at second!"

Terry, hurt by Tony's stinging public accusation, bent over, cropped a handful of grass and tossed it angrily aside. Most of the time he was able to laugh off remarks guys made about his poor throwing arm. But it was getting so that Tony's remarks always hurt.

My throwing arm is just an excuse, Terry told himself. *It's my color that Tony doesn't like.*

The Forest Lakers settled down and Woody Davis faced the next batter. There was one out and a man on third.

The pitch. Then a smashing blow to second! Jeff fielded the ball and whipped it to first. The runner on third started for home, then dashed back.

The next batter drove a sizzling line drive over Woody's head, scoring a run. A strikeout ended the Yellow Jackets' romp. Yellow Jackets 2, Forest Lakers 0.

"Get on, Bud," Coach Harper said.

Bud did. He singled to left and Ed

Caliel scored him on a triple to right center. Stu Henderson popped out and Caesar Valquez grounded out, bringing up Woody Davis. The fans cheered the young pitcher as he took the metal doughnut off the fat end of his bat and stepped to the plate. He windmilled the bat a couple of times, then stood still as he waited for the pitch. It came in and he belted it for a single over third, scoring Ed. Jeff flied out, ending the second inning.

Terry ran out to left, wondering how long he'd last if he muffed another play. Bob Decker was a utility infielder and outfielder, and Mick Jordan was able to handle an outfield position if necessary. Either one could take his place if Coach Don Harper saw fit to take him out.

Woody fanned the first Yellow Jacket, then grooved the first pitch to the next batter. The blow was a long high drive to left that made Terry get on his bicycle. He made a leaping catch that drew applause from the crowd — including some Yellow Jacket fans — and pegged the ball in to Ed. It bounced and rolled most of the way to the third baseman, but it didn't matter. No one was on base.

Jeff missed a hot drive. Then a safe hit to left field, which Terry caught on the first hop, left men on first and third. A good arm might have thrown the runner out at third, but Terry's weak throw gave him time to make it standing up.

The runners perished on base, though, as Woody struck out the next batter. Greatly relieved, Terry ran in from the outfield.

Tony led off in the bottom of the third, smashing out a double to start things rolling. Terry stepped up to the plate, then moved a few inches closer to it as Coach Harper had suggested. He waited for a pitch he liked, hoping desperately to knock Tony in, and struck out on the same pitch that had become his bugaboo — the high outsider.

"I guess that standing closer to the plate doesn't help," observed the coach. "You've just got to learn to bring 'em down, Terry. Jim Burling's got good control, and he knows your weakness."

"I've been trying," Terry confessed.

"I know." The coach patted him on the knee. "Take it easy the rest of the game. I'll have Bob Decker take your place."

"Okay," said Terry. Deep inside he was relieved by the coach's decision.

He watched Rich hit a double, scoring Tony. Then Bud singled, scoring Rich.

Those were the only runs the Lakers were able to run up that half inning. They were in front now, 4–2.

The fourth inning went by scoreless. The Yellow Jackets picked up a run in the fifth, but neither team scored again and the Lakers won, 4–3.

The guys rushed at Woody, yelling and cheering their first victory. Terry found himself among them, forgetting everything that had happened on the field, thinking only about this wonderful moment. He flung his arms around the guys and cheered with them.

Not until he felt his arm being lifted away from a shoulder did the spell break. The shoulder belonged to Tony Casterline, and the look was plain enough: *Keep your arm off me.*

6

TERRY STARTED in the game against the Roadrunners, a fiery team that wore all-white uniforms except for the picture of a roadrunner on the front of their jerseys. It was Thursday, the first of July, and the temperature was soaring in the nineties.

The Forest Lakers had first raps and Mick Jordan was scheduled to pitch. On the mound for the Roadrunners was a left-hander, Hank Rhodes.

The game got underway and Jeff Roberts, leading off, took a 1–2 count, then blasted a pitch directly at the center fielder. One out. Tony grounded out on the first pitch and Terry stepped to the plate.

Swoosh! A swing and a miss.

"Too high, Terry!" Tony shouted.

Terry grimaced. *I wish Tony would keep his mouth shut while I'm batting,* he thought angrily.

"Ball!" High and outside.

"That' a way to look, Terry!" Mick said.

Swoosh! Another swing and a miss.

"Oh, no!" Tony moaned. "He did it again!"

Terry stepped out of the box, leaned over and ran his hands up and down the smooth sides of the bat. Then he stepped in again, braced his feet and held his bat high and off his shoulder.

The pitch. It came in belt-high. Terry

stepped into it and swung. *Crack!* A bullet-piercing drive to deep left! The ball kept going . . . going . . . going . . .

Over the fence! A home run!

Terry dropped his bat and circled the bases, the cries of the fans ringing warmly in his ears. Nothing had sounded so great in a long, long time.

He was met at the plate by each player, who shook his hand as he ran by. Even Tony was there to meet him, saying, "Nice blast, Terry."

Rich flied out, ending the top of the inning.

Mick had trouble with the first Roadrunner and walked him on four straight pitches. A bunt sent the man down to second, then a line drive over second scored him. 1–1.

In the top of the second, Bud Philips

singled, Ed flied out, and Stu Henderson hit into a double play.

In the bottom of the second Mick again had trouble with his control. He walked the first man up, then redeemed himself by catching a pop fly when the next batter tried to bunt.

A drive between first and third allowed the runner to reach third base. Then, with men on first and third, the next batter delivered a solid blow to deep left that again made Terry get on his bicycle. The ball dropped over his head for a hit. He ran after it as it bounced to the fence, picked it up and heaved it as hard as he could toward the infield.

Ed Caliel, as he should have, played close to his third-base sack. Tony came out to the outfield to receive Terry's throw in, but not far enough. By the time he got

the ball and pegged it home, both runners had scored — *and so had the hitter.*

It was a home run. The Roadrunner fans went wild.

Terry stood glued to the spot from where he had pegged the ball, looking on with his legs spread-eagled. *Darn you, Tony*, he thought. *That would not have been a home run if you had come closer. You could've thrown him out!*

He didn't know how they got the next hitters out, but they did.

"I'm sorry, Mick," Terry said as he ran in and reached the pitcher's side. "That was my fault."

"Your fault, my eye," Mick said. "Tony knows you've got a poor arm. He should've run out farther for your throw."

Terry agreed, but said nothing.

The Forest Lakers soon picked up two

runs, beginning with a single by Caesar Valquez, then successive hits by Jeff, Tony and Terry. Terry had doubled, giving him a two-for-two hitting record in the game so far.

Mick held the Roadrunners hitless in the bottom of the third, and Lefty Rhodes did the same with the Forest Lakers.

It was in the bottom of the fourth that the Roadrunners started to lambaste Mick again, getting two hits right off the bat. Then Mick walked two men, forcing in a run. He had three balls and no strikes on the next batter when Stu called time, ran out to the mound and talked to Mick.

The talk hardly helped. Mick fired a strike, then grooved the next pitch too, only to see it go for a hit over short. Two runs scored and Coach Harper called time. He took Mick out and called in the reserve pitcher, Woody Davis, who had been warming up behind the third-base bleachers.

Woody pulled the Lakers through without giving up a hit, and managed to pitch the rest of the game with no Roadrunner scoring. The bats of the Lakers weren't sounding off loud enough, however, and the Roadrunners took the game, 7–3.

Terry had been up four times: knocking a homer, a double, walking once and striking out his last time up. It was the strikeout Tony Casterline remembered, for it was the last out of the game.

"You just can't get it into your head, Terry," he said with biting sarcasm. "You struck at two pitches that were way high and outside. You could've walked and saved Rich a chance to bat. We had two men on. And Rich was due to hit."

Terry looked at him. His eyes shone like hard glass. "And you could've come out farther on that hit that went up against the fence to save a run," he countered. "Why didn't you?"

Tony's face reddened. He looked around, saw Jeff, and went toward him. Mick grinned at Terry.

"That's telling him," he said.

Terry saw his father come running toward him and the boys. Behind him were Mrs. Delaney and Connie.

"Tony! Jeff!" Mr. Delaney yelled. "Lose or not, you're all invited to our place for ice cream and cake!" he said cheerfully.

Terry looked happily at his father and mother. No one could say that Dad wasn't trying to keep harmony among the boys.

"I . . . I'm sorry," Tony stammered. "I've got someplace else to go."

"Oh, that's too bad," said Mr. Delaney. "Maybe next time."

"I'll be there, Mr. Delaney," Rich Muldoon said.

"So will I," said Ed Caliel.

A similar chorus rose from the other guys, including Coach Harper, whose blue eyes twinkled. "Me, too, Mr. Delaney," he said.

"Mark," Mr. Delaney said.

Coach Harper grinned. "Mark," he echoed. "And I'm Don."

They shook hands, smiled at each other, and Mr. Delaney said, "Everybody come right over. All we have to do is put the stuff on the table."

Some of the players rode to Terry's house with Coach Harper. But most of them, including Terry and his family, walked.

There wasn't enough room for every Laker to sit at the red picnic table, so Mr. Delaney brought out a card table and chairs. Mrs. Delaney and Connie served the refreshments.

Terry looked at the group, pleased as he could be that most of the members of the team had accepted his father's invitation. Only Tony and Jeff weren't there. He wasn't surprised that Jeff hadn't come. Tony had probably influenced him not to.

A noisy vehicle came buzzing down the street, and Terry saw Harry Casterline's dune buggy pulling up to the curb. He was alone.

For a moment he sat there, the motor idling. He was gazing at the group, and Terry surmised that he was looking for Tony.

"Come in, Harry!" Mr. Delaney yelled.

"Join us for some ice cream and cake!"

Harry Casterline seemed to hesitate a while, as if considering the invitation. Then he shut off the motor and came striding across the lawn, looking sharp in a black sweater and flashy, bell-bottom pants.

"Where's Tony?" he asked curiously.

"He said he couldn't come," Mr. Delaney replied. "Wait. I'll get you a chair."

"Thanks, Mr. Delaney," Harry said. "I can stand."

His smile faded slightly as his thoughts seemed to stray — stray, Terry thought, to his brother Tony.

7

AFTER THE ice cream, cake and soft
drinks were finished, Coach Harper
and the members of the Forest Lakers
thanked the Delaneys for the treat and
left. Harry Casterline thanked them too,
then turned to Terry.

"Would you like to ride in a dune
buggy, Terry?" he asked.

Terry's eyes widened. "You bet I
would!"

"Do you mind, Mr. Delaney?"

The big man's eyes shone as he looked
from Harry to his son. "Not at all."

"Thanks, Dad!" cried Terry. "Oh — can Mick come along?"

"Why not?" Harry waved to Mr. Delaney and headed for the dune buggy. "See you, Mr. Delaney! Come on, guys!"

Terry and Mick raced across the lawn to the little vehicle. Mick climbed up behind the seat and grabbed hold of the metal guard bar. "You sit in front, Terry," he said, his face glowing with excitement.

Terry sat down in the passenger seat and buckled on his seat belt. Harry slid in behind the wheel, buckled on his seat belt, then started the motor and drove off with a roar from the twin exhausts.

"Tony say why he couldn't go to your party?" Harry asked.

"No," Terry replied. "He just said he had someplace else to go."

The dune buggy sped smoothly down

the street, turned left at the intersection and went up a steep grade.

"How are you and Tony getting along, Terry?" Harry asked.

Terry was surprised at the question. "Okay, I guess," he said half-heartedly.

"You're being modest," Harry said. "I know better. That kid brother of mine was brainwashed about black people by our parents a long time ago, and it's going to take some doing to change him. I just hope you two guys will become friends. I'd like Tony to realize that the color of a person's skin has nothing to do with what he believes in and how he lives."

"Any reason why your parents don't like black people, Harry?" Terry asked freely.

"Yes and no, Terry," Harry replied. "My parents never knew a black family.

All they knew was what they read in the papers or heard what white people said. Then my father was beaten out of a job as a construction foreman by a black guy. My father admits that the better man won, but it didn't help him see blacks as great guys. I don't know. It's a pretty complicated thing to talk about. I confess that I was like my folks until I was old enough to get away from home more and meet a lot of people, both white and black. I don't choose my friends by their race anymore."

"I wish Tony was like that," Terry said. "We'd have a real good baseball team if he was."

Harry laughed. "Yes, I suppose you would. I've seen how he plays his position when a ball is hit to you. Oh, he'll come around to seeing things differently some-day. I'm sure of it."

"I hope so," Terry said, but he thought, *I don't know. I've heard that song before.*

They reached the outskirts of Forest Lake, crossed an abandoned railroad track, and started past a dirt road when Mick shouted, "Hey, Harry! Motorcycle Hill is to our left! Ever climb it?"

"With this dune buggy?" Harry smiled.

"Yeah!" said Mick, a mischievous grin spreading over his face.

"No. But we can try it." Harry looked at Terry. "Okay with you, Terry? Motor-cycle Hill is pretty steep. It's where cycle nuts try their luck. Some make it, some don't."

Terry shrugged. He couldn't say no. He and Mick were Harry's guests. Whatever

81

Harry wanted to do was all right with him.

"Okay by me," he said.

"Fine," said Harry. "It's been something I've wanted to do with this dunie bug ever since I got her."

He pulled into a driveway, backed out and returned to the dirt road. He sped over it, gravel banging up against the fenders, till they reached a high, barren hill several hundred yards to their right. He geared down the motor and turned onto the wide road that led to the hill. The slope was about two hundred feet high and gouged from where hundreds of angry motorcycle wheels had struggled to climb to its top.

"Still game?" Harry asked.

"It's your dunie bug," Terry replied.

Harry shifted gears and started for the hill. When they reached it, the nose of the dune buggy rose as the little four-wheeler began to climb. Up, up it went, the motor roaring, the wheels spinning, kicking back dirt and gravel.

Laughter shrilled from behind Terry, and he turned to see Mick hanging onto the guard bar, his hair flying in the wind.

"Go, buggy, go!" Mick shouted gleefully.

They reached the halfway point and were still climbing. The dune buggy bounced, slid sideways, bucked like a bronco. Higher and higher it climbed, while Mick's laughter rang louder and louder. The hill got steeper. Terry felt an excitement mixed with an equal dose of fear.

He had trust in Harry Casterline, though. He was sure that nothing could happen.

But something did.

The dune buggy struck a rock that jolted its front end. The wheels twisted to the right, jerking the steering wheel out of Harry's hands. Horror-stricken, Terry felt the vehicle begin to careen over.

"Mick, jump out!" Harry shouted. "Terry, unbuckle your seat belt and jump!"

Fingers trembling, Terry unbuckled his seat belt and jumped.

8

TERRY STRUCK the ground, fell to his knees, got up, and scrambled out of the way of the overturning dune buggy. The vehicle missed him by a foot as it rolled over.

On the other side, safely out of its way, were Mick and Harry, watching the dune buggy start to roll down the steep hill. Each time the guard bar hit, the vehicle bounced high into the air, spun halfway around, struck the ground with its wheels, then bounced again.

They watched in shocked silence until

the dune buggy stopped rolling at the bottom of the hill. It shuddered and lay on its side like a dead animal.

Harry and the boys scrambled down to it. Its two free wheels were still turning.

"Boys," Harry said sadly, "I'm sorry. I — I'm just glad that both of you got out of it safely."

"I'm glad that you did, too," Terry said, still trembling.

Harry walked round to the side of the vehicle, lifted it a little, and looked at the boys. "Think we can do it?" he said.

"We can try," Mick answered.

The three of them, with Harry in the middle, combined their strength to lift the vehicle and gradually succeeded in getting it right-side up.

"We did it!" Mick exclaimed triumphantly.

"Well," Harry observed, breathing a tired sigh, "the key's still in it."

He hopped in and turned the key. *Whir! whir!* The motor burst to life. "Well, guys, that much is okay," he said. "Hop on!"

The boys hopped on, and Harry put the dune buggy in gear, stepped on the gas, and turned the wheel. "Oh, oh," he said. "The steering wheel's damaged."

With some effort he made the turn, however, and drove to the main road that led into town. There was a *bumpety-bump* in the ride that hadn't been there before, just as there were dents in the fenders and hood that weren't there before.

They drew amused glances from pedestrians and drivers on their way, and eventually pulled into a garage. Harry talked to a mechanic, then said to the boys, "Well it's the hospital for the dunie bug for the next week or two. My house is a couple of blocks away. Let's clean up, then I'll drive you home in my father's car."

At the house Terry met Tony and Tony's mother and father. All three of them looked wide-eyed with astonishment as Harry explained what had happened. Terry sensed the hostility in Mr. Casterline's eyes, and remembered what Harry had said about his parents. All they knew about black people was what they had read and heard, he'd said. Terry felt that he was being scrutinized as he returned from the bathroom.

"Well, you look better," Mr. Casterline said, smiling. "You didn't get hurt?"

"No."

"Not even a scratch?"

"No. I was lucky."

"How about you, Mick"

Mick grinned. "Just got dirty when we hopped off the dune buggy," he said, cheerfully.

"You were all lucky," Mr. Casterline admitted.

Terry hoped that the man would talk more to him; that talking would start him to realize that he was a human being first and black second, just as he himself was a human being first and white second.

Terry remembered what Tony had said about his father's having played in the big leagues, and suddenly he felt happy because, for the first time in his life, he was in the presence of a former big league baseball player.

Maybe if I said something about his

major league career he would talk a little more and forget some of those prejudices he's had against black people, Terry thought. Harry had gone into the bathroom to wash up and would be out in a minute.

Terry's heart pounded, and he forced a smile. "Mr. Casterline, I heard that you used to play in the big leagues," he said. He paused, still overwhelmed by the thought of it. Mr. Casterline was a big man — at least six foot three — and probably had knocked a lot of home runs.

A curious look entered the big man's eyes. "Who told you that?" he asked.

"Tony," Terry said.

Mr. Casterline frowned and stared at his son. "When did I ever tell you that, Tony?" he inquired.

Tony blushed. "Well, you were with

91

the Minnesota Twins, weren't you?" he said.

"No. I was with their farm team," Mr. Casterline replied emphatically.

"What's the difference?" Tony turned and headed for the outside door, but not before Terry had seen the color of his ears. They were pure red.

"Come back here," Mr. Casterline ordered.

Tony came back. His father's eyes were hard as he gazed at him. "There's a lot of difference," he said sharply. "You shouldn't have said that. You gave Terry the wrong impression." He smiled at Terry. "No, I never played in the big leagues, Terry. I was close, but never close enough."

9

THE FOREST LAKERS played the Thunderheads on Tuesday, July 6, with the Lakers having last raps. The day was cloudy, and radio reports indicated that there was a forty percent possibility of rain.

Mick Jordan, on the mound for the Forest Lakers, kept the Thunderheads hitless during the top of the first inning. The Lakers did better. Jeff led off with a walk, going to third on a double by Tony, which put the home team in excellent scoring position.

Terry stepped into the box and watched Ted Joseph, the tall pitcher for the Thunderheads, turn and squeeze the ball as if he were trying to squash it. Ted wore thick glasses, threw with a side-arm delivery, and had good control.

"Strike!" yelled the ump as the first pitch grooved the plate.

Another pitch, high and outside. The kind Terry liked. He swung — and missed. "Strike two!"

"Get 'em down, Terry!" Tony yelled from second base.

Terry stepped nervously out of the box, leaned over and rubbed his sweating hands in the dust. *Why couldn't he powder those high, outside pitches?* he wondered. *Why did they always look easy to hit?*

He brushed the dust off his hands,

grabbed the bat and returned to the box. Two men on. A good opportunity to score a couple of runs and make Tony back off his high horse.

Ted Joseph breezed in the pitch. Terry watched it anxiously. It looked good. He swung.

"Strike three!" shouted the ump.

"Oh, no!" Tony's voice boomed from second.

Head bowed, Terry returned to the dugout. He dropped his bat and sat down, shaking his head.

"You still go after those high, outside pitches, Terry," Coach Harper said. "Ted Joseph knows it, and he's got pretty good control."

"I guess I'm a real sucker for 'em," Terry admitted.

Mick, sitting beside him, socked him

gently on the knee. "Don't worry, Terry. One of these days you'll get that pitch out of your system and knock that ball all over the lot."

Terry grinned. "Oh, sure. And be another Hank Aaron. Right?"

Crack! Terry looked up and saw Rich Muldoon high-tailing it for first base. Then he saw the ball arcing toward left center field. A roar broke from the Forest Lakers' fans as Jeff Roberts crossed the plate, Tony Casterline at his heels.

Terry clapped and tried to avoid Tony's eyes as the shortstop trotted in to the dugout behind Jeff.

"Coach," Tony said, breathing hard, "did you tell Terry that he's still swinging at those high, outside pitches?"

"I reminded him," Coach said. "And he

knows it. Quit harping on it. You're not the coach here, you know."

Terry's eyes locked with Tony's. He couldn't mistake the frigid look that told him more than a hundred words.

He remembered the day at Tony's house when he had asked Mr. Casterline about his major league baseball career, and Mr. Casterline said that he had never been in the majors. He remembered the look Tony had given him then — a look mixed with embarrassment and resentment. Tony, Terry felt sure, wouldn't forget that moment for a long time to come.

Bud Philips smacked a clothesline drive directly at the third baseman, who stepped on the bag before Rich could tag up. A double play. Three outs.

Cheers exploded from the Thunderhead fans as the teams exchanged sides.

Mick lowered the boom on the first batter. The next socked a low pitch to left center for a neat double. Mick then walked two men in succession to fill the bases, and Stu called time.

The catcher trotted to the mound to talk to Mick. So did Jeff, Bud and Ed. Tony remained at deep short. Terry thought that he had never seen Tony act this way before. Tony was usually one of the first to run in to the pitcher, to help him settle down, to tell him that the situation wasn't as dark as it seemed.

This time, for some reason, Tony was staying out of it. Did the coach's remark have something to do with it? Terry wondered.

The guys returned to their positions.

The ump called time in, and the game re-sumed.

Crack! A single to right! A run scored. The second runner tried to score too, but a hard throw from Jeff to Stu, after Caesar Valquez had pegged the ball in from the outfield, threw out the runner. A pop fly to Ed Caliel ended the threatening rally.

Ted Joseph's side-arm delivery worked effectively during the bottom half of the second inning, holding the Lakers score-less. Then the Thunderheads threatened again. This time their bats thundered loudly and produced results.

Two consecutive hits to deep left had Terry scrambling madly for the ball and pegging it to third. Both times the ball had dropped far too short and two runs scored easily. Both times Ed Caliel had run out to get the ball and relay it home.

But his throws had fallen short, too. It would have taken a mighty arm to throw out a runner from where Ed had thrown it.

"Old no arm!" Tony Casterline yelled at Terry. "When are you going to trade it in?"

"Why don't you come in for the relay?" Terry shouted back. "Maybe we can throw out some of those runners at third!"

"Oh, sure!" Tony replied.

But wasn't that reasonable? Terry thought. *If Tony ran out and intercepted the throw in, Ed could cover third base. Even if the relay to him was too late to nab the runner at third, at least it would hold him on base, or get him out at home if he dared to risk running there.*

Mick fanned a Thunderhead, but that only seemed to increase their rage. Their booming bats knocked in two more runs.

"Tony!" Terry yelled. "Call time! Talk to Mick! Maybe he's too tired to keep pitchin'!"

Almost at once Tony lifted a hand and cried, "Time, ump!" The base umpire lifted his arms as a signal to the plate umpire, who lifted his arms too and called for time. The infielders ran in and huddled around Mick, and Terry's heart warmed a little. It was the first time that Tony had ever heeded his suggestion.

Then Woody Davis walked to the mound and Mick walked off. A cheer from the Forest Lakers' fans burst out for Mick, who kept his gaze glued unhappily to the ground all the way to the dugout.

There were two men on as Woody threw in a half a dozen warm-up pitches. Then time in was called and Woody went to work. He had trouble with his control and walked the first man, filling the bases. He took his time on the next hitter, and struck him out. Two outs.

The stands were silent as the next Thunderhead came to the plate. There was even silence in the infield, until Terry cried, "Come on, you guys! Get alive! Say something!"

Ed started the chatter. Tony joined in. Presently all nine men were shouting in a chorus of voices filled with spirit and enthusiasm.

The pitch. *Smack!* A sky-reaching fly to short left center field. Terry ran after it, shouting, "I've got it! I've got it!"

He heard another voice yelling too. "I'll take it!"

He was positive, though, that he had

a better chance to catch the ball, since he was running toward it. He reached for it. Just as he caught it someone collided into him and down they both went.

When he regained his senses he saw he had run into Tony.

10

"THAT WAS MY ball, Terry. I yelled for it," Tony said hotly as he sat on the ground, glaring.

"I yelled for it, too," Terry countered, rising and straightening his cap.

Tony got up slowly, and Terry wondered if he was hurt.

"I was under the ball, waiting for it, when you plowed into me," Tony went on, still fuming.

There was a shout from center fielder Rich Muldoon, and Terry realized that the teams were exchanging sides. He ignored Tony and ran off the field.

Coach Harper was standing in front of the dugout, waiting for him and Tony.

"You guys all right?" he asked, concerned.

They nodded.

"That was my ball," Tony insisted, going past the coach to the dugout. "I was waiting for it."

"He's right, Terry," Coach Harper agreed. "That *was* his ball. Didn't you hear him yell for it?"

"Yes. But I . . . Well, I was sure it was mine, too. That's why *I* yelled."

"He was waiting for it," the coach pointed out, "while you were still running. Better watch it the next time. A collision might turn out worse."

"Yes, sir," Terry promised.

"And you, Ed," the coach turned to the third baseman, "should've yelled, too. It's your job as well to let the guys know who should catch that ball."

Ed Caliel looked sheepishly at him. "I wasn't sure," he said apologetically.

"Make sure," the coach said. "Yell someone's name, even if it's just to prevent a collision. Tony and Terry were lucky that neither one of them was hurt. Okay. Let's play ball. Who's the first batter?"

"I am," Jeff Roberts said.

The wiry second baseman already had on his protective helmet. He stepped to the plate, waited out Ted Joseph's pitches, and got his second free pass to first.

The Forest Lakers' bench was like a funeral wake. Not a sound came from it even when Jeff trotted to first base. The Thunderheads' lead of 5 to 2 seemed to have muzzled the Lakers' enthusiasm.

Terry reflected on the fly ball he had gone after and the collision with Tony. He realized he had jumped from the skillet into the fire. He had given Tony another excuse to taunt him.

He saw Tony step to the plate, and remembered he was up next. He put on a helmet, selected his favorite bat, and stood beside the dugout.

Tony flied out.

Terry walked to the plate, let a pitch go by for ball one, then swung at one of those high, outside ones he liked so much. *Swish!*

"Oh, come on, Terry," came Tony's disgruntled remark.

Then *crack!* A hard blow between third

and short. Terry bolted to first and Jeff advanced to second.

Rich grounded out, however, and Bud popped to first to end the threat.

The Lakers held the Thunderheads scoreless in the top of the fourth, then rallied in the bottom half of the inning. A single by Ed, and then a triple by Caesar Valquez scored the Lakers' third run of the game. Woody's single drove in Caesar, making the score Thunderheads 5, Forest Lakers 4.

Again in the fifth inning the Thunderheads weren't able to get a man on. The Lakers came up, and Rich's long clout over the left field fence tied up the score.

With the score tied, excitement began to mount. In the sixth, Woody grooved a pitch down the center of the plate. *Boom!* The ball sailed out like a rocket to left center field. Terry chased after it, caught it on the first hop and pegged it to Rich, who relayed it to second base. The runner started past the bag, then spun and slid back to it as second baseman Jeff Roberts caught the ball and put it on him.

"Safe!" yelled the base umpire.

Jeff argued the call for a moment, then gave up and tossed the ball to Woody. Terry grinned. Jeff was a fireball when he disagreed on a decision.

A ground ball to third. Ed fielded it nicely and whipped it to first. One out.

A big right-hander stepped to the plate. Terry backpedaled a few steps. *Crack!* A hard blow to left! Terry started to run back toward the left field foul line. The ball hit in fair territory and bounced to the fence. Terry sprinted after it, picked it up and pegged it in to Ed who had run out for the throw. Ed then fired it to Tony, who was covering third, and Tony tagged the runner.

"Out!" boomed the ump.

But a run had scored. The Thunderheads were back in the lead, 6–5.

They couldn't score again and the Lakers went to bat with their backs against the wall. Caesar flied out to short. Then Woody chalked up his second hit of the game, a double. Jeff swung hard at two pitches in an effort to drive in the tying run, but grounded out to third. Tony tried hard too, and managed to draw a walk. With two on and two outs, Terry strode to the plate.

"Belt it, Terry!" Mick yelled. "Just a single's all we need!"

Terry grounded out.

11

THE FOREST LAKERS lost their next two games — to the Cornhuskers and the Boilers — and were in the doldrums.

"Chin up," Coach Harper said encouragingly. "It's not the end of the world."

For Terry it was close to it. There was a parallel between him and the team, he figured. Both were losers. There was a chance for the Lakers to start winning, but would there be for him?

Tony Casterline was still hostile toward him. The gap in their relationship hadn't closed a bit. As a matter of fact, it seemed to have widened.

On Monday, July 19, Terry and Mick were walking to the game with the Yellow Jackets when Mick mentioned something that Terry wished he hadn't.

"Did you get invited to Tony's birthday party?" he asked

Terry stared at him. "You must be kidding."

Mick laughed. "I'm sorry. He still doesn't like you, does he?"

"Not a bit," Terry said. "Sometimes I think the situation between us is worse than the first time we met."

"His father speaks to you, doesn't he?"

"He says 'Hello' when he sees me. A couple of times he even paid me a compliment. He isn't all thawed out, though. I can tell."

114

"Harry's all right, though, isn't he?"

"Oh, yes. Harry's okay." Terry remembered the day that Harry Casterline had driven him and Mick up Motorcycle Hill. "His dune buggy fixed yet?"

Mick nodded. "Saw him with it yesterday."

The game started with the Yellow Jackets taking first raps. Woody Davis was on the mound for the Lakers. It was a clear, warm day and the bleachers were packed.

Nothing happened in the first inning. The Yellow Jackets threatened to score in the top of the second as their lead-off hitter lambasted a long triple, but third base was as far as he got.

The Forest Lakers broke the scoreless tie in the bottom half of the second inning when Ed came through with a surprising triple and scored on Stu Henderson's

115

scratch single to short. Then, in the top of the third, the Yellow Jackets' bats began singing a tune that meant disaster to the Lakers. Two runs scored on back-to-back doubles. A third run scored after a hit to short left field which Terry caught on the first hop and whipped in to home in an effort to nab the runner.

The Yellow Jacket beat the throw by two steps. Terry was certain that anyone else could have thrown the man out easily. He turned unhappily and went back to his spot, waiting to hear a disparaging remark from Tony. Surprisingly, it didn't come.

A pop fly, a strikeout, and a fly to Terry ended the bad half inning.

Tony singled to start off the bottom half of the third, and Terry got the signal to bunt. He waited for the pitch, stuck out his bat and *crack!* A pop-up to the pitcher!

Tony had started to second and was sprinting back to tag up when the pitcher whipped the ball to first.

"Out!" cried the ump.

Terry stood in the batter's box, staring at Tony as he came trotting in to the dugout. Their eyes locked.

"You call that a bunt?" Tony snorted.

"I didn't say it was," Terry replied calmly.

Terry followed Tony to the dugout.

"You shouldn't have run, Tony," Coach Harper said firmly. "On a bunt you wait until the ball is on the ground. You should know that."

"Sorry," Tony muttered as he squeezed in between Caesar and Woody. Mick pushed aside to make room for Terry.

"It was my fault, too," Terry said as he sat down. "A horse could've bunted better than that."

Rick doubled to left center. Bud's fly to right ended the inning.

Nothing significant happened in the fourth. The infield seemed as quiet as a cemetery and Terry tried to put some spark into it. "Come on, guys! Talk it up! Chatter!"

They came to life. They chattered. Their voices joined together, became one. Ed smiled at Terry. "That-a-boy, Terry," he said. "That's what we needed."

Woody walked the first man in the fifth inning, then worked up to a 3–2 count on the next batter. He stepped off the mound, took off his cap, wiped his face with the sleeve of his jersey, then stepped in again.

118

Crack! A high fly to short left field! Terry sprinted after it. "I'll take it!" he yelled.

"I've got it!" another voice yelled in front of him.

He glanced down for an instant and saw Tony running back toward him. *What shall I do?* he thought. *I can't risk another collision!*

Then he heard Ed yell, "It's Tony's ball! Tony's ball!"

"Take it, Tony!" Terry shouted.

He slowed down and watched Tony catch the ball with little effort.

"Nice catch, Tony," he said, smiling.

A grin flashed over Tony's face. "Thanks, Terry," he said.

Terry trotted back to his position, feeling pretty good that this time the play had worked perfectly. Even Tony had cracked a grin, as if to say, *We did it right this time, didn't we?*

A hot grounder to Jeff resulted in a double play. Three outs.

"Come on, men," Coach Harper snapped. "This is the fifth inning and we're two runs behind. What d'you say?"

Jeff walked. Tony tried twice to bunt him down to second and fouled both times. He then hit a scratch single to short. Jeff ran to second in time to beat the throw. Two on, no outs, and Terry was up.

He glanced at the coach, saw him brush his left hand across his chest.

The bunt signal was on.

12

NERVOUSLY, Terry stepped into the box and waited for the pitch. In it came, knee high. He moved into bunting stance and stuck out his bat.

A neat bunt down the third-base line! The Yellow Jacket third baseman rushed in to field it, scooped it up and whipped it to first. Out! But both Jeff and Tony had advanced a base and were now in good scoring position.

"Nice bunt, Terry," Coach Harper smiled as Terry came trotting in to the dugout.

"Thanks," said Terry.

Rich took a 1–1 count, then singled through short. Both Jeff and Tony scored. 3–3! The Forest Lakers' bench and fans went wild.

Jeff and Tony ran in to the bench, Jeff sitting down beside Terry. He moved over to give Tony room, and Tony sat down. Both boys were breathing hard from their run.

"Nice bunt, man!" Tony laughed, socking Terry playfully on the knee.

"Thanks," said Terry.

"We've got to keep this up," Tony said, turning his attention to the ball game. "We've got to pull ahead of those guys."

"If we pull together we will," Terry said. "But we've got to pull together."

Tony looked at him. Their eyes locked

122

in heavy silence. Then Tony nodded. "Yeah, you're right. It's the only way."

The rally continued. Bud singled, advancing Rich to third, and Ed stepped to the plate.

"Drive it, Ed!" Terry shouted above the din rising from the fans.

Crack! The ball sailed over short for a single and Rich scored. 4–3! The Forest Lakers' bench emptied. The guys jumped, danced, and cheered, their cries mixing with the triumphant yell exploding from the fans.

"Keep it going, Stu!" Terry yelled. "Get a hit!"

Stu didn't, though. He flied out to left for the second out, and Caesar popped out to short for the third.

"Let's hold 'em!" Tony cried as the team

ran out to the field in the top of the sixth.

The Yellow Jackets' lead-off man laced a pitch between first and second for a double, then scored on a single to center field that drew a terrific applause from the Yellow Jacket rooters. 4–4!

Terry saw Tony grab up a handful of dust and toss it angrily aside.

"Stick in there, Tony!" Terry yelled. "Let's not give up, man!"

Tony looked at him and smiled as he lifted his hand with the V for victory sign. "We'll pull together! Okay?"

"Okay!" cried Terry, and thought, *Was the atmosphere really thawing between him and Tony?* It was hard to tell just yet.

The next Yellow Jacket popped a fly to short. One away.

Woody caught Tony's soft throw, rubbed the ball a minute, then stepped back on the mound. He checked the runner on second, stretched and threw. A solid blow to Rich in center field! He caught the fly and rifled it to third. But the runner, after tagging up at second, slid safely under Ed's outstretched glove.

"Two away!" Tony shouted, waving two fingers at the outfielders. "One more to get!"

The next hitter came to the plate and Terry took a dozen steps in toward the infield. He remembered that the hitter didn't have much power. The guy had knocked two singles, and both were shallow drives over short.

Woody mopped his brow with a handkerchief, stepped on the mound, got his signal from Stu, and pitched. *Crack!* Another solid blow over short!

Even as Terry ran in to field the ball he

saw the runner on third already sprinting for home. He wanted to shout "Tony, come here!," but realized that he didn't have to. Tony was on his way toward him.

Terry pegged him the ball, and in one swift motion Tony whipped it home. Stu caught the ball near the plate and put it on the runner as he slid in under a cloud of dust.

"Out!" shouted the ump.

Three outs! The Forest Lakers' fans thundered their unanimous approval.

Tony waited for Terry to reach him, and both ran off the field together. "Nice play, Terry!" Tony exclaimed. "You played your position perfectly!"

Terry grinned. "He hadn't hit too far before," he said. "I figured he wouldn't hit too far this time either."

"Hey, what a memory!" cried Tony.

"With my kind of arm I need it!" Terry chuckled happily.

"Yeah. I guess I'll just have to run out to left field everytime a ball is hit to you," Tony said, laughing.

The crowd gave Woody a big hand as he stepped to the plate. A moment later they let out a sad "Ah! Too bad, Woody!" as he popped out to short.

Jeff didn't do any better, grounding out to third for the second out.

"Come on, Tony!" Terry cried as Tony stepped to the plate. "Get on!"

Electric silence charged the air as Tony waited for the first pitch to come in. It blazed in chest high and he swung. *Crack!* The ball streaked past the pitcher to the outfield for a single and once again the Forest Lakers' bench clambered out and cheered with gusto.

127

"Get a hit, Terry!" Tony yelled from first base. "Get a hit!"

Terry felt the sweat on his hands as he gripped the bat and waited for the pitch. It came in, but it was high. *No!* a voice inside him warned. *Don't swing!* He let it go by.

"Ball!" cried the ump.

The next pitch was lower. It grooved the heart of the plate and Terry swung. The blow was solid and sounded like music to Terry's ears. He saw the ball sail like a rocket out to deep right center field. Even as he dropped his bat and bolted to first he heard the victorious cheer erupting from the Forest Lakers' fans. He crossed first, second, and was held up by the coach at third.

Then he saw the fans spilling out of

the stands, and the guys running toward him, led by Tony himself.

"Nice smash, Terry!" Tony cried, pumping his hand. "You won the ball game, man!"

Terry blinked happily. "Like we said . . ."

"I know," Tony interrupted. "We have to pull together. And we did, didn't we?"

Terry nodded.

After the shouting and handshaking were over, Terry and some of the other guys picked up the bases and equipment and put them into the canvas bags for the coach, then headed for home.

"Terry, I — I don't know how to say this," Tony said uneasily, "except that I'm sorry."

"Why? Because I hit that triple?" Terry laughed.

"No. You know what I mean."

Their eyes met for a moment, and Terry nodded silently.

"I'm having a birthday party at my house next Saturday," Tony said. "I'm inviting the whole team. I hope you can make it."

Terry felt a lump lodge in his throat. He had been hoping that Tony would invite him. He grinned and poked his new friend on the shoulder.

"Try and stop me," he said, and turned to see Mick smiling happily at them.

How many of these Matt Christopher sports classics have you read?

Baseball

- ❑ Baseball Pals
- ❑ Catcher with a Glass Arm
- ❑ Challenge at Second Base
- ❑ The Diamond Champs
- ❑ The Fox Steals Home
- ❑ Hard Drive to Short
- ❑ The Kid Who Only Hit Homers
- ❑ Little Lefty
- ❑ Long Stretch at First Base
- ❑ Look Who's Playing First Base
- ❑ Miracle at the Plate
- ❑ No Arm in Left Field
- ❑ Shortstop from Tokyo
- ❑ The Submarine Pitch
- ❑ Too Hot to Handle
- ❑ The Year Mom Won the Pennant

Basketball

- ❑ The Basket Counts
- ❑ Johnny Long Legs
- ❑ Long Shot for Paul
- ❑ Red-Hot Hightops

Dirt Bike Racing

- ❑ Dirt Bike Racer
- ❑ Dirt Bike Runaway

Football

- ❑ Catch That Pass!
- ❑ The Counterfeit Tackle
- ❑ Football Fugitive
- ❑ The Great Quarterback Switch
- ❑ Tight End
- ❑ Touchdown for Tommy
- ❑ Tough to Tackle

Ice Hockey

- ❑ Face-Off
- ❑ The Hockey Machine
- ❑ Ice Magic

Soccer

- ❑ Soccer Halfback

Track

- ❑ Run, Billy, Run

All available in paperback from Little, Brown and Company

Join the Matt Christopher Fan Club!

To become an official member of the Matt Christopher Fan Club,
send a self-addressed, stamped envelope (10 x 13, 3 oz. of postage) to:

Matt Christopher Fan Club
34 Beacon Street
Boston, MA 02108

Books by Matt Christopher

Sports Stories

Animal Stories

The Fox
Steals Home

The Fox
Steals Home

by Matt Christopher

Illustrated by Larry Johnson

Little, Brown and Company
BOSTON   TORONTO   LONDON

Library of Congress Cataloging in Publication Data

Christopher, Matthew F.
  The fox steals home.

  SUMMARY: Already troubled by his parents' divorce,
Bobby Canfield is further distressed when he learns that
his father, who has coached him in running bases, intends
to move away.
  [1. Baseball—Fiction. 2. Divorce—Fiction]
I. Johnson, Larry, 1949–   II. Title.
PZ7.C458Fp   [Fic]   78–17526
ISBN 0–316–13976–9
ISBN 0–316–13986–6pb

HC: 10 9 8 7
PB: 15 14 13 12

MV

*Published simultaneously in Canada
by Little, Brown & Company (Canada) Limited*

PRINTED IN THE UNITED STATES OF AMERICA

To Ed and Naomi

The Fox
Steals Home

One

STEP BACK, Bobby. Let's go for two."
A pause. "Bobby! Wake up!"

The voice woke Bobby Canfield from his thoughts, and he looked at Coach Mark Tarbell, the tall, thin man standing near the right-side corner of the Sunbirds' dugout.

Bobby stepped back to the grass behind third base, suddenly conscious of the Cowbirds' batter that had just come to the plate. A kid in a uniform too large for him, with one pantleg hanging lower than the other.

Bobby's face colored slightly. He should have made that move without being told, but he had not been quite himself lately. It had been hard to concentrate on baseball

3

with all the trouble that had gone on back home.

He glanced over his shoulder at the scoreboard, and saw that it was still one out and the top of the third inning. So far both teams had nothing but goose eggs showing in the black squares.

"Pitch it to 'im, B. J.!" yelled Andy Sanders at first base. "He's nobody!"

"Lay it in there, B. J.!" Bobby chimed in, spitting into the pocket of his glove.

Try as he might, he couldn't shake off the thoughts that kept plaguing him. His mother and father's divorce papers had been filed only a few days ago, and it was like a bad dream. Every once in a while he felt almost convinced that he would wake up from it, but he had reached the point now where he knew it was no dream. It was all real.

"Come on, Bobby!" yelled second baseman Eddie Boyce. "Look alive there!"

Look alive? How could he when he felt so lousy?

He took notice that there were runners

on first and second, and vaguely remembered the sizzling grounder and the scratch hit that had got them on.

"Ball!" boomed the ump as B. J. breezed in a pitch.

"Don't walk him, B. J.!" pleaded Billy Trollop from center field.

B. J. laid his next pitch across the inside corner.

"Steerike!" announced the ump.

The Sunbirds exploded with approval. The fans with theirs. It was a hot June day, ideal for the shirt-sleeve crowd. Ideal for everyone except Bobby, to whom these last few days had all seemed the same. Terrible.

"Strike two!" said the ump as the batter swung at another pitch and missed.

Sherm Simmons tossed the ball back to B. J., who stepped off the mound and rubbed the ball a bit before getting back on the rubber again.

Checking the base runners, and then quickly shifting his attention to the batter, B. J. chucked in his next pitch.

Crack! It was a low bouncing grounder to Bobby's left side! Sprinting after it, he caught it in his outstretched glove, and snapped it to second base. Eddie Boyce was there, made the catch, and whipped it to first.

A double play! Three outs.

The fans applauded, and the Sunbirds praised Bobby for the play. He blushed slightly as he ran into the dugout and laid his glove on its roof. He liked the sound of that applause. It was the kind of music he could listen to anytime.

He wished he would hear another voice, too. That not-too-loud, mildly excited voice of his father's.

A couple of times during the game he had glanced at the crowd, hoping to spot the yellow cap that was his father's trademark. He hadn't seen it, and a sadness had crept into his heart. He wondered if his father would ever come to see him play again.

"Hey, Bobby! You're up, you old glove man, you!" grinned Eddie, picking up a bat

out of the upright rack. Eddie was second batter in the lineup. Bobby was first.

Bobby selected his bat, a yellow one with a taped handle. He put on his helmet and stepped to the plate. This was about the time he would usually hear that familiar voice of his father's ringing out, a cheerful sound that was most encouraging, especially when he needed it.

How much he wished he could hear it now.

He looked at Walter Wilson, the Cowbirds' big right-handed pitcher. After two innings of acute observation, Bobby figured him to be somewhat arrogant.

He let the first pitch go by. It was in there for a strike.

The first time at bat he had flied out to center. This time he hoped to even things up a bit. It would be awful to get up tomorrow morning knowing that he had played his first game of the season and hadn't gotten a single hit.

Walter stretched, jerked out his left foot,

came around with the ball, and winged it. It was in there, letter-high and straight as a string.

Bobby swung. *Crack!* He met the ball on the fat part of his bat and saw the white blur streak over second for a clean hit. A good, triumphant feeling went through him as he dropped his bat and sprinted to first.

He glanced at Walter, and saw the Cowbirds' pitcher picking up a handful of dirt. Rising up, the big boy tossed it disgustedly back to the ground.

I guess that hit got to him, thought Bobby, a hint of a smile on his lips.

He looked at the third-base coach, and couldn't believe what he saw — thumb to cap, to belt, to chest, and back to cap. The steal sign was on!

He sucked in his breath. What a surprise! He had never stolen a base before!

Well, he loved running the bases. He was fast. He had always outrun Billy Trollop in a sprint.

He waited for Walter Wilson to step into

the pitcher's box, then took a four-step lead. He stood, crouched — and sped back safely as Walter whipped the ball to first.

The first baseman tossed the ball back to Walter. Again Walter got on the mound, checked Bobby carefully, then delivered.

Bobby took off, losing his helmet halfway down the base path as he ran as fast as he ever had. Just as he neared the bag he saw the Cowbirds' second baseman reach for the ball, catch it, and bring it down for the tag.

But, in his anxiety to tag Bobby, the second baseman moved too quickly. Never having had complete control of the ball, he dropped it.

"Safe!" yelled the base umpire.

An enthusiastic cheer exploded from the Sunbirds' fans as Bobby rose slowly to his feet and brushed off his pants.

His father would have liked that. Yes, sireee.

After retrieving his helmet Bobby again

glanced at the third-base coach. This time it was finger to cap, to chest, back to cap, and then to belt. The bunt signal was on.

Eddie went after the first pitch. His position for bunting was perfect, but his execution of it wasn't. The ball popped up to the third baseman, who then zipped it to second before Bobby could tag up. It was a quick, surprising double play that left Bobby bewildered.

For the second time he rose with dirt-smeared pants. As he ran across the diamond to the front of the dugout before brushing himself off, he didn't fail to notice the smug look on Walter Wilson's round, sweaty face.

"Way to go, Walt!" yelled the Cowbirds' third baseman. "Let's take the next one! He's no sticker!"

Billy Trollop, the Sunbirds' third batter, made the player eat his words on the first pitch as he walloped it between right and center fields for a double. Andy Sanders repeated the feat, driving his two-bagger down along the left field foul line, scoring Billy. As if that weren't enough to prick Walter Wilson's ego, Snoop Myers belted a single over short that scored Andy.

That called for a consultation with Walter around the mound. It involved all four infielders and the catcher, each of whom presumably suggested to him how to handle the situation.

It probably did some good, for the next batter, Toody Goldstein, drew a walk. Then Hank Spencer flied out, ending the four-hit, two-run inning.

The teams exchanged sides, the Sunbirds standing somewhat more erect and looking self-assured now that they were enjoying a 2–0 lead.

Bobby, however, wasn't very happy about getting picked off at second base. He thought that if he'd had his wits about him he would have waited to see where the ball was going.

He could just picture his dad looking at him after that dumb play and saying, "No use being sore about it. It's over. Just try not to let it happen again."

He knew it wasn't his father's disposition that had been the cause of his parents' breakup. Nobody in this wide world had a more pleasant disposition than did his father. And it wasn't drink, the way it had been with Mr. Blake who lived down the block. Oh, Bobby's father had a glass now and then, but never enough to intoxicate him. He just didn't care for the stuff that much. As a matter of fact, neither did Bobby's mother. It was other things that had caused the lousy breakup. Their interests. Their priorities.

"Watch for the bunt, Bobby," cautioned Coach Tarbell.

The thoughts dispersed as Bobby glanced at the batter, a kid with hair the color of washed carrots. He bent his knees, let his arms dangle loosely at his sides, and suddenly imagined he was Pete Rose, Graig

Nettles, and Buddy Bell all rolled into one. He was sure that nothing was going to get past him. He was a staunch wall, able to stop anything that came his way.

B. J. pitched. *Crack!* A smashing line drive directly to the shortstop.

One out.

Well — what difference did it make where the ball was hit? As long as it was caught.

The next batter popped up to first.

"You're in the groove, B. J.!" Bobby yelled.

The Cowbirds' third batter came up, a small kid with blond curls sticking out from underneath his helmet. He let two pitches sail by him, one a ball, the other a strike. Then he laid into the third pitch as if he really meant it. The *smack!* of bat connecting with ball was solid. So was the hit, a sharp single over Bobby's head. Not even with a ten-foot ladder would he have been able to nab that one.

He stepped back, forgetting the famous triple personalities all rolled into one that

14

he had imagined himself to be. Right now he was just Bobby Canfield, the not-so-famous third baseman for the not-so-famous Sunbirds.

Two

*B*J. WALKED the next batter, and a hopeful hum started among the Cowbirds' fans. They cheered as their next hitter stepped to the plate, a look of anxiety on his round face. He was chubby, and his helmet sat high on his head, leaving the ear-protective section almost too high to do any good. He held his black bat about four inches from the end of the handle, and waved it like a club.

Boom! B. J.'s first pitch went skyrocketing to deep right center, scoring both runners. Chubby, not blessed with lightning speed, had to be satisfied with a double.

It was all tied up now, 2–2. The Cowbirds were making a gallant comeback with two outs.

"Let's get back in the groove, B. J.!" yelled Bobby, spitting into his glove as he crouched in his spot at third.

"Take yer time, B. J.!" advised Snoop. "Take yer old time, boy!"

B. J. didn't have to be told to take his time. He had been doing that. He had seen lots of games on television in which the pitcher dilly-dallied on the mound, dug and redug the dirt around the rubber, wiped the sweat off his face, hitched up his pants and then studied the catcher's signs for five minutes before going about his business of pitching the ball. B. J. was already a vet in that department.

The kid in the uniform that looked two sizes too large for him, with the uneven pantlegs, came up. Bobby remembered the smashing grounder he had driven down to Snoop that Snoop had muffed. This kid was no slouch with the bat.

"Not too good to him, B. J.," said Bobby quietly.

B. J. checked the runner on second — more out of habit than because he expected the chubby guy to steal third — and delivered the pitch. It was high and inside.

His next pitch was almost in the same spot. His third was low for ball three.

Nervously, he began digging at the mound with the toe of his shoe, wiping the sweat off his face and hitching up his pants again. Then he studied Sherm Simmons's sign, which Sherm displayed with the professional aptitude of a Johnny Bench. Nodding agreeably, B. J. got into position and pitched.

It was down the middle for a called strike.

He tried to repeat the pitch, and grooved it, but this time Baggy Pants laid into it for a long triple to deep center field. The drive gave Chubby plenty of time to make it home for the Cowbirds' third run.

Somehow Bobby wasn't surprised about

18

the hit. Baggy Pants might not have cared how he looked in his baseball uniform, but as a player he was one hundred percent.

Two pitches later, a fly ball that must have climbed as high as the Empire State Building, almost disappearing out of sight, came down and was misjudged by center fielder Billy Trollop. The hitter got two bases on the hit, and credit for an RBI as the fourth run scored.

The fifth run came on a grass-scorching single between third and short. The third out finally came on a strikeout, which drew the loudest applause since the game had started.

B. J. walked off the mound with his head bowed. Until he reached the dugout he was a lone kid. Nobody said as much as a word to him.

When he sat down, Coach Tarbell offered him a few words of baseball wisdom. "Chin up, B. J. They just had a hot inning. No reason why we can't come back and do the same thing. Okay, Sherm," he said, turning to the catcher, who was stripping off his leg guards. "Let's start it off."

The back of his shirt sweat stained, Sherm walked to the plate and did just that, pulling a base on balls. B. J., not the best hitting pitcher in Lyncook County, bunted him down to second. The third baseman, who fielded the bunt, threw B. J. out at first.

Bobby got up from his kneeling position in the on-deck circle and strode to the plate, carrying his bat like Reggie Jackson. He looked eyeball-to-eyeball at the pitcher like Reggie Jackson, and swung like Reggie Jackson. But he missed twice.

Then Walter threw him a slider. The ball looked like the head of a snake coming around a tree. It headed for the plate, and Bobby swung again.

Crack! The ball sizzled out to short. The shortstop made the play to first, and Bobby was out. Sherm advanced to third.

Bobby made the turn to the right and trotted back to the dugout, completely forgetting that he was Reggie Jackson. Maybe he ought to try being Graig Nettles the next time.

Eddie slam-banged a double, scoring Sherm, and kept alive the Sunbirds' hopes of overtaking the Cowbirds. But Billy Trollop got up and pricked the balloon with a pop-up to third.

Cowbirds, 5–3.

Bobby looked across at Walter coming off the mound. The pitcher was squinting over his shoulder at the scoreboard in center field. Then he turned and looked grimly ahead. He was probably pondering a way to keep that lead, thought Bobby.

B. J. laid the first batter to rest with a strikeout. The next batter popped a high, towering fly over third base. Bobby got under it, feeling nervous all of a sudden as the ball started to play tricks on its way down. But he held out his glove, and he had it. Two outs. Then as he waited for the third batter to step to the plate, his mind began to wander.

You must try to see it from my point of view, too, Bobby. I'm your mother and I love you. You're my only child, the only good thing I have left. You must realize that your father and I just can't keep on living together like this. We'd be hypocrites to continue living together just because some people think that it's the proper thing to do. Well, it isn't, Bobby sweetheart. It's not the proper thing to do at all. Why, you can see for yourself how insufferable your father and I are getting to be toward each other. We're not happy and you're not happy. And it'll just be getting worse and worse, Bobby sweetheart.

The words were a fuzzy sound in the far recesses of his mind. There were tears in her eyes when she had spoken them, tears that had brought an ache to his throat.

The third batter lashed a furious drive past B. J.'s legs that sizzled out to center field for a single. And Bobby broke his daydream and began to fret. Another run would mean that the Sunbirds would need four runs to knock off the Cowbirds. And in this game the Sunbirds didn't seem to have that many left in them.

"Take 'im yourself, B. J.!" shouted Bobby.

The next batter grounded out.

"Amen," murmured Bobby as he relaxed and trotted off the field.

"What inning is this, anyway?" B. J. asked as he plunked down on the dugout bench.

"Bottom of the fifth," said Coach Tarbell. "Andy! Snoop! Come on, you guys! Grab your bats! Start it off, Andy!"

Andy did — a corking single over first. Snoop bunted him down to second, sacrificing himself, although he made a gallant effort to turn the bunt into a hit.

Toody Goldstein, batting left-handed, looked sick on the first two pitches, missing both by inches. Then he connected with a fast pitch that drove Andy in for the Sunbirds' fourth run. Toody stayed on first, clapping proudly. It was his first hit of the season.

Hank Spencer stepped to the plate and began nudging his left shoe into the dirt as if he wanted to bury it. He took a called strike. Then Walter came back with another pitch that headed for the heart of the plate. It was a mistake. Hank laid into it, and the sound of bat meeting ball was music to the Sunbirds' ears.

It went for a home run.

On the mound, Walter's shoulders drooped as if something had happened to his collarbone.

"Send him to the showers!" yelled a Sunbirds devotee.

Sherm flied out to left, and B. J., who wasn't much with the stick, anyway, grounded out to short.

Sunbirds, 6–5.

In the top of the sixth, the Cowbirds connected with two hits, one walk, and two runs, to forge ahead, 7–6.

"Come on, Bobby!" encouraged Coach Tarbell as Bobby walked to the plate to start off the bottom of the sixth inning. "Let's get that run back — and more!"

Images of Graig Nettles, Pete Rose, and Buddy Bell floated through Bobby's mind as he strode to the plate.

Walter gazed at him through narrowed lids, stretched, and delivered. The pitch was wide. "Ball!" snapped the ump.

Bobby fouled off the next two.

Then Walter seemed to have lost sight of the plate, and Bobby walked.

Bobby trotted to first, then looked across the diamond at the third-base coach, who was watching Coach Tarbell standing at the side of the dugout. Whatever the sign was that Coach Tarbell related to the third-base coach Bobby didn't know. But the sign directed to him was clear as the hot shining sun.

Thumb to cap, to belt, to chest, back to cap. The steal sign was on.

Oh, man! Well, grease your joints and gas up your tank, Bobby. You're going to move!

Walter stepped on the mound, looked over his shoulder at Bobby, then started his delivery. Bobby took off, dirt puffing from his heels as he sprinted toward second base. Just before he reached it he saw the Cowbirds' second baseman covering the bag, waiting for the throw from his catcher.

Bobby hit the dirt, slid, and touched the bag a second before the Cowbird touched him with the ball.

"Safe!" called the ump.

On the mound Walter Wilson looked on, not liking the call one bit.

Three

*B*OBBY TRIED not to show it, but deep inside he was as proud as could be.

He wished again that his father was there, that his father could have seen him run. But, as before, the thought of his father reminded him of the divorce.

Why couldn't you two get along like millions of other married people? Why did it have to happen to us?

Bobby was nuts about baseball. But right now he was never happier to see a game coming to an end. It was a wonder that he had played as well as he had, because worrying about family problems had taken a lot out of him. And he hadn't been able to concentrate at the most crucial times.

"Drive 'im in, Eddie!" he heard Toody Goldstein yell. "Tie up the score!"

Who was to blame for the mess? His father or his mother? He didn't know. How could he? He didn't know every little thing that had gone on between them. No kid would. You didn't see everything. You couldn't hear everything.

Let's be careful about this, you and me. We don't want him to worry his little head over our problem. This is strictly between you and me, see?

That was the way the mess — the whole rotten mess — had seemed to exist to him. He didn't know when the smelly business had started. That was pretty difficult to tell. But it had been about a year ago when he had begun to see the signs: the cold tone of voice between his mother and father, the angry questions, the angry answers. Then the hours of awful silence, which were even worse.

Bobby shut out the ugly thoughts and concentrated on the batter, Eddie.

Eddie took three swings, striking out, and walked off the mound, his lips pursed.

Billy got up and popped up to third. Andy Sanders grounded out to second, leaving Bobby stranded.

Neither team scored in the seventh, and the game went to the Cowbirds, 7–6.

Eddie's parents came off the stands and hugged Eddie for the double he had hit. Andy's father came down and shook Andy's hand for the three hits he had pounded out. Hank's parents and his two sisters came down and hugged him for the single and the colossal home run he had smashed. Almost every one of the guys had somebody meeting him either to congratulate him on his hits, offer sympathy for losing, or both.

No one was there to meet Bobby. His mother wouldn't meet him of course. She didn't care sour apples for baseball. Or, he thought, for anything he did, for that matter.

"Hey, Bobby! Tough game to lose!" said a voice out of all that maze of voices.

Bobby looked around in surprise and saw that it was Mr. Trollop, Billy's father.

Bobby tried to smile. "That's right, Mr. Trollop," he said.

He walked home with some of the crowd, not saying anything to anyone, because no one said anything to him. He might as well be on the street alone.

"A broken home." That was a term he used to hear now and then at school, at play, and occasionally at home. It had meant very little to him. "Hey, Jimmy! Hear about Dave's parents? They broke up!" The usual response was "That right? Tough." Or, sometimes more frankly, "Oh? So what else is new?"

But, since the terrible thing had happened right in his own home, a "broken home" had suddenly taken on a definite meaning. For a long, long time there were the three of them — his mother, his father, and himself. And then one day he woke up and there were just the two of them — he and his mother.

It was too hard to believe.

There was a court trial about something to do with custody, a trial that had made him wish that he had never been born. Not that there was any violence between his mother and father. No, it was nothing like that.

It was just the strained calmness that had gone on between his parents, his mother's lawyer, and the judge. His father had not wanted a lawyer to represent him. He had said that he knew beforehand who would take custody of Bobby, and he was entirely agreeable to it.

It was that darned agreeableness that had bothered Bobby so much, because sometimes he felt that he loved his father more than he did his mother, even though he knew that the right thing to do was to share his love equally between them. That was hard to do sometimes, because both of them were so different. They had different interests. She liked partying, cards, bazaars, things that his father didn't care a hoot about. He was an outdoorsman. Give him a gun, or a fish pole, and a free weekend in the mountains, and you wouldn't find a happier man.

How the two of them had ever gotten together and married was beyond Bobby's imagination. And having him, their only child, must have just complicated the unimaginable union.

He arrived home, and saw a car parked at the curb — a shiny white car with tinted glass, chrome trim, and a CB antenna sticking straight up from the middle of the trunk. It was a car he had never seen before. Only a person rolling in dough would sport such luxurious wheels.

Bobby paused in his tracks and looked at the house. It was an old, two-story building that his father had renovated from an old two-story shack. Somebody had said that it had first been constructed as the village post office. That was only thirty years after the signing of the Declaration of Independence.

Whose car is it? he wondered. *A salesman's? An insurance man's?* It could be any one of a dozen people who might want to see his mother.

Maybe it was her lawyer's, Mr. What's-his-name. Hugo Ferris. But why should he want to see her again? The case was over, wasn't it? Well, maybe he just wanted to drop by and see how she was doing. A short, gray-haired man in his sixties, he had that warm, sympathetic quality about him that Bobby's mother seemed to have needed.

Or it could be one of her bridge-playing friends. She had a lot of them. Maybe they were having a chitchat, "woman talk," as his mother called it. His mother usually got home from work at ten after five, so whoever it was visiting her couldn't have been here very long.

He walked onto the driveway, noticing his mother's banged-up Chevrolet in the garage, and walked past the house toward the lawn in back. A hundred feet beyond was the lake, a spacious body of water covered with gently rolling waves and an array of sailboats and motorboats.

A three-foot-wide dock extended out to a hoist in which an inboard-outboard motorboat sat like a setting hen. It used to be Roger Canfield's favorite mode of transportation to various fishing spots on the lake. Since he had left, the boat had not been touched, although Bobby knew how to run it almost as well as his father did. He just hadn't felt like taking it out, that was all.

He sat on the edge of the dock and watched other boaters and water-skiers skimming across the lake, having the time of their lives. He had waterskied a few times himself. Man, it was fun. But that was before the breakup. Maybe, when he felt like it again — when the turmoil and the pain of his parents' divorce were behind him — he could get Billy Trollop and some other guys and go waterskiing again.

After about ten minutes, he thought about going up to the house. He was hungry, and his mother was probably expecting him, anyway.

When he reached the side of the house and looked around to the front, he saw that the white car was gone.

Well, if it were Mr. Ferris, the lawyer, his mother would have enjoyed the visit. He was an old guy, smart as a whip, but with a subtle sense of humor that would help Bobby's mother forget her cares for a while.

On the other hand, if it were somebody like Mrs. Trundle — that gossipy woman who used to be a neighbor and had moved to another part of town — Bobby's mother might have welcomed an earlier appearance by him.

Well, he didn't like to bother her when she was having company, that was all.

He entered the house through a side door, closing the door quietly behind him.

"Is that you, Bobby?" his mother's soprano voice carried to him from upstairs.

"Yes, Mom. It's me," he said.

"I'll be right down, dear," she said.

He went to the living room and started up the stairs to his room. He was only half-way up when she emerged from her room, wearing a bright yellow dress and high-heeled shoes, and carrying a small white purse.

"Bobby sweetheart!" she cried. "You look terrible!"

She stopped on the steps and brushed back his hair.

"You better get that uniform off and take a shower," she went on hastily. "And use a lot of soap."

"Where you going?" he asked her. He didn't remember her telling him that she was going somewhere this evening.

"Where am I going?" She stared at him as if that were the number-one dumb question of the day. "It's my bridge night, dear. I told you that this morning. Didn't I?" she added, a frown suddenly forming on her forehead. "Oh, I'm sorry, dear. Maybe I didn't. Anyway, it's Tuesday night, and you should know by now that I have a bridge party every Tuesday."

He looked at her pensively, wondering if she would tell him who her visitor had been.

But she didn't. She was too much in a hurry to leave. She just told him to get washed up, put on clean clothes, and to find his dinner in the oven.

"What is it?" he asked. He hoped it wasn't beans and corn again. He was getting tired of beans and corn.

"Spanish rice," she said, smiling.

He smiled back. Spanish rice he liked.

Four

HIS MOTHER woke him up the next morning at 7:15.

"Gee, Mom," he cried, looking sleepily at his Mickey Mouse alarm clock. His father had bought it for him when he was eight, and it was still ticking along as merrily as ever. "It's the middle of the night!"

"You know what time it is," she replied, her voice coming up the stairway in one giant leap. "Get your b-o-d-y down here, so you can wash up and eat breakfast. You've got only fifteen more minutes before I have to leave."

"Why can't you leave without me?" he

retorted. "I can make my own breakfast. All I eat is cereal, anyway."

"This morning I want you to have eggs," she said. "Protein is good for you. Now come down here and don't argue with me."

"O—kay," he said.

He shoved off the covers, rolled out of bed, and silently dropped upon the floor. The hardness of it was unbearable. But he lay there awhile, his eyes closed, until his back began to ache. Then he got up.

The sun was shining brightly through the curtains of his window, proving that it and the clock were both working against him. He dug clean socks and underwear out of his dresser, put them on, then put on his pants, shirt, and shoes, and went downstairs. He managed to do it without falling, which was somewhat remarkable since he had kept his eyes closed all the way down.

"Well, good morning, bright eyes," said his mother, who was already dressed in her work clothes and ready to go. She was a secretary in an office, and her work clothes were a trim-fitting dress and high heels. The rest of her outfit — a white, goatskin jacket that Bobby's father had bought for her two Christmases ago — was lying over the back of a chair.

" 'Morning," said Bobby, heading for the bathroom.

"Scrambled or sunny side up?" shouted his mother while he was washing his face.

"Sunny up!" he replied, finding it an effort to raise his voice enough to get it through the door.

After a while he managed to get dried and out of the bathroom. His sunny-side-up eggs, atop a piece of dark toast, were waiting for him, along with extra toast and a glass of milk.

"I want you to go to Grandma's today," said his mother as she pulled on her white jacket. "You don't have a baseball game again today, do you?"

"No," he said, sitting down on the chair

in front of the eggs. "Our next game is Thursday. Why do I have to go to Grandma's?"

"I want you to, that's why."

"When do you want me to go?"

"Sometime this morning. At least before lunch, so you'll have something else besides peanut butter and jelly for a change."

Grandma Reenie makes good peanut butter and jelly sandwiches, too, he almost told her.

"Good-bye, dear," his mother said, kissing him on the forehead. "See you this afternoon."

" 'Bye, Mom," he said, and watched her go out of the door.

While he ate he heard the old Chev grinding away in the garage as his mother tried to start it. It suddenly sparked to life, then roared madly as his mother pressed down on the accelerator. *That's right, Ma*, he thought, smiling to himself. *Goose it. Clean out the carbon good, and maybe burn up the rings one of these days. Can't you remember Dad warning you about that?*

He finished his breakfast and put the dishes into the sink. Then he stared at them a while, pondering whether to wash them or not. One part of his brain told him he didn't have to, the other part advised him that he should.

He got to thinking about his mother struggling all day in front of a typewriter, typing up a pile of letters for her boss till her fingers were sore. And he grinned. *Oh, sure,* he thought. *I know that mother of mine better than anybody else does. She would never type so much to ever get her fingers sore.*

Nevertheless, the other part of his brain won. He did the dishes.

When he was finished he went into the living room and headed for the AM-FM stereo set. He'd put on an old Paul McCartney record, he thought, and then get the baseball scores.

His attention was drawn to the ashtray

on the coffee table. He had forgotten about his mother's visitor, but apparently whoever it was smoked, too, just as his mother did. He stared at the stubs of two cigarettes, one that he recognized as his mother's brand, the other, which was different. It had a tan band around the tip of it.

Suddenly he was Sherlock Holmes investigating the clue of the tan-banded cigarette stub. *Come on, Watson. Let's take a closer look and see what's elementary about it. Shall we, old boy?*

He stepped closer to the coffee table, and made a unique discovery. Both stubs had lipstick stains on them. Well, at least it wasn't a man. That would leave out the lawyer, Mr. Ferris. But that was as far as his investigative powers were able to go. He had determined that his mother's visitor was a woman: that was all.

For Mom's sake, he thought, *I just wish it wasn't Mrs. Trundle. That old bag of wind would talk the ears off of anyone who would listen to her. And Mom would listen to her even though she would never take Mrs. Trundle seriously.*

Glancing at the clock, he saw that it was nine-thirty. News time, followed by the baseball scores, would be coming on shortly. He didn't care about the news, but he had to listen to the scores. Music and sports. Without them you could throw your radio out the window.

At twenty-five minutes of ten he turned on the radio, heard the last bit about a railroad train derailment somewhere in Illinois, then the all-important, team-by-team scores in both the American and National leagues. The Yanks topped Boston. The Orioles downed the Brewers. The Oakland A's just eked out a victory over the California Angels.

He kept staring at the brightly lighted dial, looking at it as if hypnotized, while he listened to the rundown of the scores.

"The Mets three, the Cardinals two. Los

Angeles eight, the San Diego Padres one." The voice droned on, clear, monotonous.

His thoughts drifted to yesterday's game, and he saw himself hitting the old apple, getting on base, and sliding into second.

Man, he enjoyed running the bases, and making that steal. There was something especially challenging about it. Hey, Joe Morgan! Lou Brock! Watch out! There's a new base stealer on the way up!

"The Reds took it on the chin, five to four, from the Houston Astros, after winning four straight—"

"Oh, no!" Bobby cried, slamming his fists against the air.

After a while it was over, and he shut the set off. He took a quart bottle of orange juice out of the refrigerator, poured himself a glass, and drank it. Returning the bottle to the refrigerator, he wiped his mouth with his shirtsleeve and picked up his baseball cap. Blue, long brimmed, it was a symbol of his life's career.

He left the house, making sure that all the

doors were locked and that the key to the side door was placed on the lamp beside it.

Grandma Reenie and Grandpa Alex Morris lived on German Creek Road. To get to it you had to go up the road for a mile or so, then turn off to the left for about another half mile. It was a long, tiresome walk. By the time Bobby arrived he wished he had never started.

"You oughta have a bike," suggested Grandpa Alex, peering at Bobby through his trifocals. Balding, and gray around the edges of his hair, he still stood up straight as a pole and walked with the graceful bearing of a soldier.

"Mom thinks there's too much traffic where we are for me to have a bike," said Bobby.

"Pooshwah! It's a wonder she didn't worry about you walking up here."

"Are you hungry, dear?" Grandma Reenie asked him. Faint lines webbed the corners of her hazel eyes.

47

"No thanks, Grandma," he said.

"I've been meaning to telephone you, Bobby," said Grandpa. "But your grandmother keeps pestering me with one foolish job after another. How did your team make out yesterday?"

"We lost," said Bobby. "Seven to six."

"Lost?" Grandpa said it as if the word had a terrible taste to it. "How did you do? Get any hits?"

"One," replied Bobby. "And one walk. I also stole a base."

"You did?" A wide grin splashed over the old man's face. "Good! You're pretty good with the stick, are you?"

"Fair."

"Fair? That's not enough, boy. You've got to be good at something, get what I mean? If not with the stick, then with catching the ball. Otherwise you won't be worth more than a lick. What would you like to be good at?"

"Stealing bases," said Bobby.

"Stealing bases?" Grandpa's jaws dropped a few notches. "Why? You a whiz on bases?"

"No. I just like to run."

"Oh. So you just like to run. Well, I suppose it's the runners that score, isn't it?" He grinned warmly.

"That's right," said Bobby.

Five

I'VE GOT A theory about life, Bobby,"
Grandpa said, focusing his eyes through
the upper third of his glasses at his grand-
son. "And that is it's best to specialize in one
thing, at least. Two or three things are
better, but could be more difficult. So, *at
least* one thing. Get what I mean?"

Bobby nodded. Anyway, he *thought* he
got what his grandfather meant.

"What I'm saying is that if you want to
be a base stealer, go all out at it. Be good
at it. Be the best. Look how long Ty Cobb
held the base-stealing record. Then Maury
Wills comes along and breaks it. Then some-

body else comes along and breaks his. Why? Because they made a specialty of it, that's why. Get what I mean?"

Again Bobby nodded. He had known that his grandfather enjoyed baseball, but he had never dreamed that the old man was so psyched up about it. It was as if he wished he were young again himself to show Bobby what he was talking about.

"Practice is the key, Bobby," Grandpa Alex went on, emphasizing the word *key* to let it sink in. "Like everything else, a guy has to practice at his craft to be the best. Why work at anything if that isn't your aim? Get what I mean?"

Bobby grinned. "I get it, Grandpa," he said. He hadn't thought about being the best in anything. But, the way Grandpa put it, it didn't sound bad at all.

"Okay. Tell you what we'll do," said his grandfather. "I'll fetch my gloves and a ball, and we'll go to the ball park. We'll stop at your house first for you to put on your baseball pants. Okay?"

Bobby nodded.

"Okay. Come on. We can put in about a half hour's practice, then come back and rest up before lunch." He turned and looked at Grandma Reenie sitting on the porch, crocheting an afghan. "Did you get all this chatter, Grandma?" he asked her. "Bobby and I are going down to the ball park. I'm going to make this kid into the best base stealer in Lyncook County."

"Just as long as you don't teach him to steal anything else," Grandma Reenie said, glancing up through her glasses but not missing a stitch. "And be back by lunchtime. I'm making chicken and dumplings."

"Half an hour. That's all we'll be gone," said Grandpa Alex.

He went into the house and stayed so long that Bobby began to wonder if he were ever going to find the gloves and bat. But he came out eventually, carrying them. They looked at least a hundred years old. *Well*, figured Bobby, *if they worked then, they should work now*.

They got into Grandpa Alex's green sedan and drove to Bobby's house, where he put on his baseball pants. Then they drove to the ball park that was about a mile toward the village, next to the school.

A few kids were knocking out flies with a softball in the outfield, but the infield was clear.

Bobby noticed his grandfather glancing toward the road now and then, as if he were expecting someone. But he thought no more about it as Grandpa Alex began issuing orders.

"Okay. Let's get down at first base. The first thing you'll need to learn is how to take your lead. It all depends on the pitcher, of course. That's the cheese you have to keep your eye on every minute. And if he's a lefty, you've got to be that much more alert. Get what I mean?"

They walked to first base. "Okay," said Grandpa Alex. "You're the runner, I'm the first baseman. Say there's a right-hander pitching. Okay. Take your lead."

Grandpa Alex stood in front of the first-base bag with one of his gloves, a bald-headed, skinny Dwight Evans. "Okay. He's looking over his shoulder at you. Now he's looking at the batter. He's throwing. Go!"

Bobby took off, slipped, almost fell.

"Come back, come back," ordered Grandpa Alex, not too kindly. "You stripped your gears, the worst thing you can do when you're stealing bases."

A car drove into the parking lot next to the first-base bleachers. Grandpa Alex saw it and flashed a knowing smile.

"Let's hold it a minute, Bobby," he said, watching the driver emerge from the car. "We've got some help."

Bobby sucked in his breath as he recognized the old blue car and the tall, middle-aged man wearing a yellow cap coming toward them across the field.

"Dad!" he said. An ache came to his throat.

"That's why you were so long in the house, Grandpa! You were telephoning Dad!"

Grandpa Alex's smile broadened. "That's right, Bobby. I knew he worked nights, so I thought I'd have him come over and give us a hand. You don't mind that, do you?"

"No. But you know what could happen if Mom finds out, don't you?" Bobby answered, fear taking the place of the warmth that had glowed in his eyes for that brief moment. "She can make him stop seeing me entirely."

"Pooshwah," snorted Grandpa Alex. "That's just a threat, that's all. Hi ya, Roger," he greeted his son-in-law with an outstretched hand. "Glad you could come."

"I wouldn't miss it for the world," said Roger Canfield. His brown eyes fastened warmly on his son. "Hi, Bobby. How you doing?"

They shook hands. "Good, Dad." Then his father wrapped his arms around the boy and held him for a minute. Bobby kept his eyes closed, giving his father squeeze for squeeze. *Oh, I love you, Dad!* he thought. *I really love you very much!*

They pulled apart, Bobby blinking his eyes slightly, then smiling at his no-holds-barred, cunning grandfather.

"Thanks, Grandpa," he said.

Even after the personal preliminaries were over, Bobby was still somewhat worried that his father was willing to risk their weekend get-togethers. But maybe his father figured it like Grandpa Alex did. Maybe he didn't think that Bobby's mother would carry out the threat, either, if she saw the two of them together now.

But how could she see them? She was cooped up in that air-conditioned office, typing up something for her boss. They were safe as money in the bank.

"So you want to be a base stealer, do you?" said his father. "And a darned good one, which is the only kind. Okay. Get on first base. Grandpa, how's your throwing arm? I know your eyes aren't the very best."

"Never was better," lied Grandpa Alex, who had played baseball until arthritis had incapacitated him at the age of forty-three.

"Okay. Get behind home plate and take that ball with you. You're going to try to throw Bobby out as he runs to second base."

"Eewowwwww!" yelled Grandpa Alex as he trotted like an old but nimble race horse to the position behind the plate. He was in baseball heaven.

Bobby, leading off the first-base bag, waited for his father to give the word. Suddenly it came. "Okay, Bobby! Go!"

Bobby took off as if he were catapulted. His father waited a moment, then yelled again, "Throw it, Alex!"

Grandpa Alex threw it. The ball got there a moment before Bobby did, except that it was about ten feet short. Bobby went into the bag standing up.

"Oops! Lost my target!" said Grandpa Alex.

"That isn't all you've lost," replied Roger, grinning. "But that's all right. The important thing is that it still is something for Bobby to run against. But next time slide, Bobby. Hit the dirt as if it's a close play.

You know how to slide, don't you? A little on your side and your knees a little bent. And come in hooking the base with your foot. You know all that?"

Bobby nodded. "I've done it before, Dad."

"Good. Okay, get on first. Try it again, and slide this time."

He tried it again, and Grandpa Alex tried to heave the ball farther, succeeding by about eleven inches. Bobby slid into the bag, hooking it with his right foot. All the major leaguers in the world couldn't have done better.

"Hey, kid!" exclaimed his father, his eyes glowing with pride. "You're a pro!"

Bobby grinned as he got up and brushed himself off.

"I want to get real good at it, Dad," he said.

They rested for a few minutes, then went at it again.

A car drew up slowly along the street, paused awhile, then accelerated and went on its way. The car didn't look familiar, nor did the man behind the wheel, but Bobby got worried, anyway. He still feared his mother's threat, even though his father and grandfather didn't seem to worry. She had meant every word she had said about his father's not being allowed to see Bobby at any time during the weekdays. Saturdays and Sundays yes, but not weekdays. It was in the papers that way, the papers that Mr. Ferris had filed away in his black satchel.

Six

*L*ET'S TRY something different," suggested Roger Canfield. "I'll get on the
mound and pitch. It might work out better
that way."

He strode to the mound, while Bobby
got into a runner's position on first base. His
father looked ten feet tall there, and like a
real pitcher as he stretched up his arms,
brought them down, then furtively glanced
over his shoulder at Bobby.

Bobby took a long lead, crouched, ready
to spring the instant his father made the
initial motion toward home.

Suddenly his father took his feet off the

rubber, twisted to the left, and made a quick throwing motion to first. Bobby raced back and stepped onto the bag, a wide grin spreading over his face.

"Would've had you," said his father. "That ball was right there in front of the bag."

"And if I was ump I would have called him safe!" boomed Grandpa Alex.

You knew where his heart lay.

Two kids came up and lay on the grass about ten feet from the foul line. They had long, straggly hair and wore moth-eaten, printed t-shirts. After glancing their way five or six times, Bobby finally made out what the printings were. One read I'M A MARTIAN, the other LOVE ME LOVE MY MONSTER.

Their presence began to irritate him, made him self-conscious. He thought that their watching him was preventing him from putting his best effort into his runs to second base. But his father offered no hint that he had slowed up.

Mr. Canfield had him running to third base, too, reminding him that there was no law against stealing the hot-corner sack if he could.

"Hey, man! You steal bases like a fox steals chickens!" one of the long-haired kids piped up.

"Yeah, you're some quick, sly fox," remarked the other.

A fox? Bobby conjured himself having a long snout and a long, flowing tail. He grinned. *Oh, sure, man!*

Another car slowed up on the street. Once again the premonition welled up in Bobby that the driver might recognize him and his father, squeal to his mother like a CIA spy, and drop the bomb that would separate him and his father. Again he didn't recognize the car, but the female driver looked familiar. Could she be one of his mother's bridge-playing friends? Or one of her bazaar friends? His mother was involved in so many things, she must have had a million acquaintances.

At last Grandpa Alex said that they had better call it quits, or Grandma Reenie would make him sleep with the chickens. They had gone way over the half-hour limit — by twenty-five minutes to be exact — and it was really high time they got back.

Bobby and his father shook hands again, reminding each other of their get-together Saturday morning at nine sharp, then started on their separate ways.

"Hey, Fox! Think you can steal a base like that in a game?" one of the kids yelled at Bobby as he started off the field with his father and grandfather.

"I'm going to try," he replied.

"I'd like to see you try it against Walt!" the other kid said. "Bet you'll never steal against him again!"

If I did it before, I'll do it again, thought Bobby. *Well, at least I'll try to do it again.*

As a matter of fact, he told himself, after the kind of workout he had just gone through with his father and grandfather, stealing against Walter Wilson should be as easy as ABC.

"See you at the next game, Fox!" the other kid promised.

Bobby smiled and waved. Fox, he thought. What a name they had tagged onto him. Crazy guys.

He and Grandpa Alex stopped at his house on their way to Grandpa's home. He changed back into his other clothes, then rode on up to his grandparents', wondering just how angry Grandma Reenie might be, because they had returned later than promised.

It would be something if she made Grandpa sleep with the chickens. The image of his grandfather snuggling down among all those hens and roosters made Bobby smile.

As it turned out, she never mentioned it, though she did appear slightly put out that they were nearly an hour late for lunch.

Bobby showered first, then his grandfather did, and it wasn't until he sat at the table that he realized how famished he was. He had two big helpings of chicken and dumplings, and then a triangle of strawberry pie, all of which filled every nook and cranny of his belly.

"You won't be able to eat tonight," Grandma Reenie said as she collected his empty plates.

"You wanna bet?" Grandpa Alex said, small eyes twinkling.

Bobby smiled. He felt like a stuffed sausage, and didn't think he'd be able to eat for a week. Anyway, his mother undoubtedly had someplace to go tonight and wouldn't have the time to make a big supper. Since the separation she kept herself so busy it seemed they never sat down to a big supper anymore.

It turned out that she didn't go out, and that she didn't make a big supper, either. Maybe it was because Bobby told her what he had eaten for lunch. "All that for lunch?"

she ranted. "What got into that crazy head of your grandmother's, anyway? She seldom cooks for lunch. In that case, it'll be canned stew tonight. I can stand a rest from cooking after slaving in that hot office all day. Whew!"

"Hot?" he said. "I thought it was air-conditioned."

"Not this week it hasn't been. The air-conditioning unit has been kaput and Lord knows when it'll be working again."

The woes of a working mother. Wonder if I'll work in a hot or an air-conditioned office when I get a job? Bobby asked himself. *Never. Not if I can become the best base stealer of the year and pull in a couple million bucks. Then retire when my legs give out, say at thirty.*

They played the Finches on Thursday under a boiling hot sun. For two and one-half innings it was a pitcher's battle, both hurlers managing to keep the batters hitting the ball into the mitt of a defensive player just as if it were planned that way. Ollie Hitchcock, the Sunbirds' right-handed pitcher, so self-conscious of his height that he walked slightly stoop-shouldered most of the time, seemed to become more erect each time he strode off the mound.

"Let's change those eyeballs to numbers," said Coach Tarbell, referring to the zeroes decorating the scoreboard. "What do you say, Ollie?"

Ollie seemed not to have heard him as he rummaged around the bat rack for his favorite home run slugger, found it, and walked to the plate. Ollie, who wore glasses and wanted to be a concert pianist when he grew up, slugged the first pitch to short for the first out.

Here we go again, thought Bobby as he left the on-deck circle and replaced Ollie's position in the batter's box. He tried to conceal his nervousness by pretending he was Graig Nettles, gripping his bat so hard that his knuckles shone white. Sixty feet away

68

from him, standing like a gargantuan on the mound, stood Bung Sweeney, the Finches' ace right-hander.

Bung fired two pitches that the ump called strikes, getting well ahead of Bobby to be able to waste a couple.

But the next pitch was in there, too, and Bobby swung. *Crack!* The ball hopped like a rabbit through the hole between third and short, and Bobby was on.

Glancing at the third-base coach, he got the sign he was hoping for. The steal sign.

"Hey, Fox! Let's see what you can do now!" yelled a voice from the first-base bleachers.

Bobby didn't have to turn around to see whose voice that was. It belonged to one of the two long-haired kids who had watched him practice base stealing. He should have known they would be here today.

Bung got on the mound, stretched, looked over his shoulder. Bobby, leading off as far as he dared, waited for that right moment, that split second that could make the difference between success and failure.

Swiftly, Bung stepped off the rubber and whipped the ball to first. Bobby got back, hardly a fraction of a second in time.

"Watch it, Bobby," warned Snoop Myers, the first-base coach.

The first baseman tossed the ball back to Bung. Once again Bung got ready to hurl, and Bobby got ready to run. This time Bung fired his pitch in, and Bobby took off. Dirt sprayed from the heels of his shoes as he sprinted for his target, second base. He lost his cap and helmet as he slid into the bag, hooking it with his foot long before the second baseman tagged him with the ball.

"Yay! Thataboy, Fox!" yelled the long-haired kid, as other fans joined in with a chorus of cheers.

Bobby rose to his feet, brushed himself off, and looked toward the third-base coach, Hank Spencer. Hank was looking toward the bench, getting the sign from Coach Tarbell. In a moment his attention was back to Bobby. He went through some crazy signs that meant nothing, indicating that Bobby was to play it safe.

Eddie Boyce, batting, slammed a two-one pitch over second, and Bobby raced to third and then home as if a dozen bears were on his tail.

Billy Trollop grounded out, but Andy Sanders kept the spark alive by blasting a double to deep left. The Finches' left fielder rifled the ball in to third as Eddie touched the bag and headed for home.

"Hey, get back, you idiot!" Hank yelled at him. "Get back here!"

Seven

*T*HE THIRD baseman whipped the ball home just as Eddie slid on his posterior in a valiant effort to bring himself to a stop. Reversing direction, he half ran, half crawled back to the bag. With a last gallant effort he stretched out his hand and touched the bag a fraction of a second before the Finches' third-sacker caught the ball and tagged him.

"Safe!" roared the base umpire.

The third-sacker stared at the ump. "What?" he shouted, started to argue, then seemed to have second thoughts about it and turned away.

"You goon," said Hank to Eddie, who had risen to his feet and was brushing the dirt off his pants. "Didn't you see me signaling you to stop?"

"I thought you were signaling me to keep going," said Eddie.

"Oh, man," Hank moaned, striking his forehead with the flat of his hand. "I'm going to get you a pair of glasses."

Snoop Myers lashed a liner through second for a clean single, scoring both Eddie and Andy. Then Toody struck out.

Finches 0, Sunbirds 3.

"Hey, Fox, you did all right!" yelled one of the kids as Bobby sprang from the dugout and headed for his position at third.

"Thanks." Bobby grinned. He had at least two good supporters, that was for sure.

Someone sitting on the third-base side of the bleachers chuckled. "Nice steal, Bobby."

The sound of the familiar voice struck a sensitive chord, and Bobby glanced toward the bleachers. It was his father! He was sitting there in the fourth row, wearing that familiar yellow cap.

"Thanks, Dad," his heart answered.

He was thrilled and surprised to see his father there. It was something he had hoped for, but not really expected.

The Sunbirds kept the Finches from scoring, and it looked as if the Sunbirds would go through the inning scoreless, too, as Hank flied out and Sherm fanned. Ollie Hitchcock, whose ability as a hitter had not ever been a major threat to any opposing team, stepped up to the plate.

Bung got two strikes on him, and was on his way for his third strikeout as Ollie went into his third consecutive swing. But this time a resounding crack exploded as bat met ball, catapulting it through the hole between left and center fields. The unbelievable became believable as Ollie made it to second base standing up.

"Knock him in, Bobby!" encouraged a fan as Bobby strode to the plate.

He felt comfortable and confident, none

of that nervousness he had felt the first two times up. That 3–0 lead could do that for you.

Bung whistled two pitches by him, both balls, then wrangled in a strike. The fourth came in knee high and Bobby swung, meeting the ball squarely for a single over short. Ollie raced in to home, boosting the lead another notch.

Bobby looked for the steal sign, eager to give his legs another workout. He stood there, some five feet away from the first-base sack, leaning forward, both arms swinging loosely. Since he had decided to excel as a base thief, nothing was more important anymore. Nothing, that is, as far as baseball was concerned.

But he didn't get the steal sign. Apparently Coach Tarbell wanted him to play it safe.

Eddie stroked the first pitch to center field for the third out. Discouraged because he was deprived of his chance to attempt another steal, Bobby trotted to the bench, got his glove and headed to his position at third.

He took a quick glance at his father, who met his eyes and smiled.

The Finches, coming up for the top of the fifth inning, still could not find the handle of Ollie's pitches, and went back out to the field, a bunch of defeated sad sacks.

Again the Sunbirds picked up a run as Andy scored on a triple to deep left off the bat of Snoop Myers. The Finches, unable to find the magic that would give them any momentum at all, picked up only horse collars again in the sixth and seventh innings, and the Sunbirds walked off with the win, 5–0.

The first thing Bobby did was head for his father, who descended from the bleachers and met him near the first row.

"Three hits and a stolen base," said his father happily. "Congratulations. You're playing like an old pro."

The third hit had come in the sixth inning, giving Bobby three-for-four for the day. His mind easily tallied up the percentage: .750. If he continued hitting like that he'd be the envy of the league.

"It's my best game so far," said Bobby proudly. "But it's only my second," he added, smiling.

"Yeah. Well, you'll do all right in the rest of them, too," his father assured him. "You've got the spunk. That comes first. All the rest will follow."

A voice cut in. "Hey, Bobby! You coming?"

It was Billy Trollop, walking toward the gate with his parents and another couple.

"I've got to go, Dad," said Bobby, anxious to keep talking with his father, yet fearful that if his mother found out about it she would try to sever their relationship forever.

"Bobby, wait," said his father. "I've got something to tell you."

Bobby started away, his heart on a cloud for being able to see his father for just that brief moment.

"Tell me about it Saturday, Dad," he said.

"I've got to go now."

"But, Bobby, that's what I want to tell you about."

Bobby stopped, his heart suddenly pounding. He waited for his father to continue, afraid of what he was going to hear.

"I won't be picking you up on Saturday," said his father. "I promised to go fishing with some buddies of mine. We were in high school together, and we haven't seen each other in years. You understand, don't you?"

Bobby's heart stopped, and he felt riveted to the ground, unable to believe what he had just heard.

"But you know that Saturdays and Sundays are—" he started to say. He couldn't finish. The words choked in his throat.

Understand? Sure, I understand, Dad, he wanted to say. *You'd rather fish with your friends than be with me!*

Well, go ahead! Don't let me interfere with your fun. I'm just your son. You don't have to keep a lousy promise to your son.

Go ahead. Go fishing. Have a good time, Dad.

"Hey," said Billy, as Bobby stopped beside him. "You okay?"

"Yeah, sure. I'm okay."

I'm fine. Just fine.

I wish I were dead.

"Where are you going?" his mother asked him.

"I'm going to take the boat out for a while."

The instant he spoke he realized how bitter he sounded. But he didn't apologize. He didn't feel like apologizing to anybody this morning, not even to his mother.

"Well!" she said. "And a good morning to you, too. What's eating you? Would it have something to do with your father?"

He had the porch door open, letting in the cool, morning breeze that was blowing from the lake.

"That's right. He's not going to pick me

up this morning. He's going fishing with some of his buddies."

"He *what?*"

He started out the door.

"Bobby! Come back here!"

He stepped back into the house, closed the door, but didn't look at her. She had her hair up in curlers. Every Saturday morning she had her hair up in curlers, whether she was going anywhere that evening or not.

"What's this about him going fishing with his buddies?" she asked, her eyes focused on him like blue agates.

"He told me that."

"When did you see him?"

"Thursday. At the game."

"Is that so?" she said, suddenly ruffled. "Even after he agreed not to see you during the week."

"Well, I saw him there, and after the game I went over to talk to him a minute." Bobby felt that he should be truthful about it. "So you can't blame him for that."

She kept looking at him. "No, I suppose if that's the way it was, I can't blame him."

She was silent a while.

"Okay if I go now?" he asked, anxious to get out of there.

"I suppose so," she said stiffly. "Since it's what you want to do."

Eight

*H*E WENT DOWN to the beach and walked out on the narrow dock. Unlocking the large wheel at the side of the hoist, he gently lowered the boat into the water. It was a sixteen-foot, fiberglass Starcraft with a 110-horsepower engine that lay exposed in the stern. The cover for it was in the small beach house up on shore.

The boat was not in top-notch shape because, like a lot of other things he kept promising to do, Roger Canfield had kept promising he'd fix the gas line running from the tank under the forward deck to the carburetor, but never had taken the time to do it. The leak from the brass fitting had become a sore Bobby had become accustomed to, and since it had not caused any trouble so far he had practically forgotten about it.

He inserted the key into the ignition, started the engine and backed the boat out of the hoist. Some ten yards out, he shifted the throttle gently forward, and got the boat moving ahead. The lake was a little choppy, causing the craft to rock. Shoving the throttle harder forward forced the bow to raise up high and the boat to speed over the water, shooting sheets of spray on either side. In a moment the bow settled down to where it belonged.

He drove toward the middle of the lake, noticing other powerboats cutting a swath through the water, too; and sailboats whisking silently along, stitching their way through the crests and troughs, puffed-out sails holding the boats in that limbo space just short of keeling over. Bobby had never sailed before, but someday he would like to.

He turned to the left, and then to the right, weaving a crazy pattern of waves behind him. With the throttle wide open, the noise from the engine was so loud he wouldn't have been able to hear himself talk if he tried.

But he didn't care. He had to do something to get the thought of his father out of his head.

He turned the wheel sharply to the right, putting the boat into a ninety-degree angle, and almost panicked as he found himself heading directly into the path of an oncoming powerboat. That boat, too, was speeding at full throttle — or near it, judging by its sound.

Quickly Bobby spun the wheel to the left, as the other craft turned to the right. Even so, both crafts veered so close to each other that very little daylight shone between them. Bobby, feeling like a fool, couldn't blame the anger he saw on the other driver's face.

Oh, man, he thought. *I'd better head back for home before I ram this boat to kingdom come.*

He turned the wheel till the bow of the boat was aimed in the direction of home, then straightened it out.

The ride, instead of erasing the unpleasant thoughts of his father, had almost resulted in a disaster. He couldn't win.

He finally reached the hoist, cranked the boat up on it, and took the key into the house. His mother wondered why he was back from his ride so soon. "Just had enough of it," he said, bending the truth somewhat. No sense worrying her about what almost happened. She might never let him go out alone in the boat again.

He had barely hung the ignition key on a nail in the laundry room when he decided to keep on going through the front door for a walk to Meadow Park. There was usually some action going on there — a scrub ball game, tennis, something.

"Now where are you going?" his mother

asked as she looked at him from the dryer where she was removing a load of clothes.

"Out," he said.

"Out where? Do I have to squeeze every word out of you?"

"Meadow Park," he said.

"Okay. You're going to be back by lunch-time, I hope."

"I'll try," he said, his voice not any friend-lier than hers.

He opened the door and went out.

I don't know, he thought. *I'm twelve and she keeps treating me as if I were still eight or nine. When will I ever be a grown-up to her?*

Meadow Park was about half a mile away. It was located on a piece of land jutting out into the lake, and contained a picnic area besides the playground for the kids. As Bobby had suspected, a baseball game was in progress — with a tennis ball instead of a baseball — and at first glance he recognized most of the kids who were playing.

Then his attention riveted on the tall

right-hander on the mound. Even though he wasn't wearing his monkey suit, he looked familiar. He was Walter Wilson, the Cowbirds' pitcher.

"Hey, there's Bobby Canfield!" yelled Nick Tully, another player for the Cowbirds. "Come on, Bobby! We're lacking a man!"

He hesitated, wondering whether to play or not. In a minute he consented. "Where do you want me?" he asked.

"On third," cried Nick. "Hey, Tommy! Get out to center field, will you?"

Tommy Elders, a regular for the Swifts, a team that the Sunbirds were scheduled to play next, ran out to center field, and Bobby took over at third. One thing about playing baseball with a tennis ball, you didn't need a glove.

He could hardly believe that he was playing on Walter Wilson's team. Walter Wilson, the Cowbird's crack pitcher.

A pop fly was hit to first, then a fast-hopping grounder was hit to Bobby. He did a Pete Rose fielding job with it, and heaved the ball to first. Unlike a Pete Rose throw, though, the ball took off like a rocket, sailing over the first baseman's head.

"Hey, man! What an arm!" yelled Toody Goldstein, covering right field.

"Moon's only five foot two, not ten foot eight!" exclaimed another Sunbird, Eddie Boyce.

Nothing like a bad throw to invite insults, thought Bobby. *Good thing it was just a scrub game.*

A towering fly ball to center ended the half inning. Bobby walked off the field, his mind still on the wild throw to first. Scrub game or not, such gross throws preyed on a guy's mind. Just because you tried to do your best in a real game, there was no reason in this wide world why you shouldn't try your best in a scrub game, too.

"Bobby!"

The voice came from someone near the lilac bushes flanking the road behind the ball park.

Bobby turned, and stared in surprise. It was his father!

"Dad!" he cried.

What was he doing here? He was supposed to be with his friends. Fishing.

His thoughts went topsy-turvy. The sight of his father twisted things all around for him.

His father motioned to him. Reluctantly, Bobby approached him.

"I stopped at the house," his father said. "Your mother told me you were coming here."

"I thought you went fishing," said Bobby.

"I called my friends," said his father. "I'm meeting them tonight, instead. Is that okay?"

Bobby's heart went up to his throat. "Sure is," he said.

"What do you want to do? Stay here and keep playing with the kids, or do something else? Anything."

Bobby thought a minute. "Can I practice base-stealing a bit?" he asked. "This would be a good time. The ball park's probably empty. I think that most of the guys are here. Then we could see the Giants play the Foxes. If you'd like to."

His father smiled. "Why not? Come on. We won't need a ball. Just your legs."

Bobby yelled to Nick. "Nick, I've got to go. Sorry! Thanks for letting me play."

"Okay!" Nick yelled back.

Bobby turned back to his father, saw him gazing attentively at one of the players.

"See somebody you know, Dad?" he asked.

"Well — yes. But never mind. Come on."

Instinctively, Bobby glanced over his shoulder, and met the strong, silent gaze of Walter Wilson. Was he the one at whom his father had stared?

But why him? How in this world could his father know Walter?

He pushed the thought to the back of his mind as he turned and followed his father to the car.

They drove to the ball park. Bobby had

guessed right; there was no one there. He practiced running the bases, getting the jump on the pitcher, and stealing second and third.

When he got tired, he rested and once suggested to his father, between breaths, that they ought to have a stopwatch.

"No way," replied his father. "You're not training to be a professional, or for the Olympics. This is just to teach you the right way to run and steal bases, and to develop those abilities as you keep playing. I don't want you to strain, either. Too much of this stuff at one time could injure a muscle, hurt you for life. We don't want to take a chance on doing that."

They had barely started practicing again — the last time today, his father promised, before they would head for the city park to see the ball game — when a car drove up slowly and parked at the curb behind the high wire fence. There was a woman in it: a stranger, at least to Bobby.

The horn honked. Bobby looked at his

father. "She honking for you, Dad?" he asked wonderingly.

His father, standing on the pitcher's mound, looked over his shoulder.

"Darn," he said, half under his breath. "What does she want?"

Nine

I'LL BE RIGHT back," he told Bobby, and walked briskly across the diamond to the car. He talked with the woman for a few minutes, then came back. The woman started up the car and took off.

"Okay," said his father, back on the mound. "Get on first. We'll go through it once more, then head for the game."

His attitude had changed. Bobby could tell by the sharp way he spoke, by the expression on his face. Had something the woman had said to him bothered him that much? Who was she, anyway?

But Bobby didn't ask his father who she

94

was. He didn't think it was his business to pry.

Finished with the base-stealing practice, Bobby brushed himself off as thoroughly as he could and got in the car with his father.

"You're probably wondering who that woman is," Roger Canfield said.

Surprised that his father should mention it, Bobby shrugged. "I don't care who she is," he said.

"She's a friend," explained his father, nevertheless. "A widow. Met her at a bowling party."

"That's okay, Dad. You don't have to tell me about her."

He didn't want to hear about her. The less he knew the better. He still had hopes of his mother and father's reuniting again sometime when the dust from their marriage problems had settled. Maybe that was looking for a miracle, but he hated to see another woman enter his father's life, making sure that the miracle would never happen.

They drove to Municipal Park and got

there a few minutes before the Giants–Foxes game started. They stayed the full nine innings, even though it was one of the dullest games Bobby had ever seen in his life: 1–0, in favor of the Foxes. And that single run by virtue of an error. Super super dull.

"Fast game, but Dullsville," said Bobby as they drove out of the parking lot.

"You should've said something," said his father. "We would have left earlier."

"I was just hoping for something to happen," said Bobby. "But nothing did."

His father laughed.

"Are you still going to church with your mother?" his father asked after a brief silence.

"Nine o'clock every Sunday," answered Bobby.

She was almost fanatic about it. She never missed.

"Good. You never know when you'll need someone to lean on, someone other than a mere human being. Know something? I just bought one of the best sellers ever published."

Bobby didn't know much about best-sellers, except for something like *Charlotte's Web* or *Fog Magic*, kids' books that his father had probably never heard of. Or books on famous athletes. He gulped them down like cereal.

"I don't know any best-sellers, Dad," he admitted.

"You know of this one," replied his father. "It's the Bible."

Bobby looked at him, a little embarrassed. "We've got one, but I've never read it. It's pretty long."

Roger Canfield shrugged. "I know, but I've been reading one chapter at a time, and I'm about a third done with the book already. Can you believe it? Me reading the Bible? I bet if your mother heard about it she'd flip."

His dad didn't press about the Bible reading, but Bobby could tell it meant something special to him.

They stopped at a red light. "There's a fair on in Meadville. Like to go there tomorrow?"

"I'd love it," said Bobby.

"Fine. I'll pick you up at the usual time, eleven o'clock."

Bobby had the sudden fear that their day had ended, that his father was going to take him home. But two blocks farther on, Roger Canfield turned right and pulled up in front of a diner.

"I'm starved, aren't you?" he said.

Bobby grinned. "Something like that," he admitted.

He enjoyed these little surprises that his father often pulled on him. They made their stay together so much more fun.

They went inside, found a vacant booth, and sat down. Roger Canfield took off his yellow cap, set it beside him on the seat, and surveyed his son. "It's been a great day, Bobby," he said happily.

"Sure has, Dad," replied Bobby. "Wish we could do it every day."

"Me too."

Idle talk. Wishful thinking. Even before his mother and father had split up, he and his father hadn't spent a heck of a lot of time together. But he was around, at least. And they often had indulged in their own private talk, which included sports, a topic his mother had placed at the bottom of her list of favorite subjects.

They ordered from a menu that a waitress brought them, and took their sweet old time putting the food away. When they were finished Roger Canfield left a tip for the waitress, paid the check, and followed Bobby out of the door.

"Feel better?" he asked.

"I'm stuffed," confessed Bobby.

His father drove up to the house at a minute of eleven on Sunday morning, picked up Bobby, and drove to Meadville, twelve miles away. The fair was already in full swing: the ferris wheel revolving slowly, every chair occupied; the stiff, plastic horses

of the merry-go-round jumping up and down in slow motion; rockets spinning in a wide circle; a fat man wearing a derby four sizes too small for him selling helium-filled balloons. On the midway, hucksters on makeshift stages were trying to inveigle the people into their tents to see "the famous chicken woman," "the alligator man," and "the two-headed goat."

"Interested in something like that?" Roger Canfield asked his son.

Bobby shrugged. "Oh, I don't know." He wasn't sure if he was or not.

"Come on," urged his father. "Most of this stuff is a lot of baloney to separate people from their money. But if you've never seen one of these shows before, now's the time."

They bought tickets to the "famous chicken woman" show, and saw a small, thin woman whose chest protruded like a chicken's and whose skin resembled a chicken's.

"I expected to see feathers," said Bobby.

"Maybe she's been plucked," his father chuckled.

The "alligator man's" somewhat brown, scaly skin was undoubtedly what had earned him his title. Bobby left the tent disappointed, although he hadn't known what to expect. An alligator man with a long snout and a snapping tail? *That's* an alligator, man!

"Had enough?" asked his father.

"Had enough," echoed Bobby.

They rode on the ferris wheel and the rocket, and tried winning prizes at the various concession stands. By evening, when they ended the day by eating a light dinner of hamburgers, salad, and ice cream, Bobby's prizes were an accumulation of sorts — a rag doll, a plastic cat, a bamboo cane, and a glass coin bank. The items were practically worthless, but they were souvenirs just the same of a day that he would remember for the rest of his life. Today was the day he had gone to the Meadville Fair with his father.

Roger Canfield drove him home, and hugged him tightly before Bobby got out of the car.

"Thanks, Dad," said Bobby, trying to keep a lump from rising to his throat. "I've had a real great time."

"So have I, Bobby," said his father. "See you next Saturday."

"Right."

When Bobby got to the door of the house he found it locked. He located the key on the lamp near the door casing, unlocked the door, and went in.

On the kitchen table was a note: *Dear, I won't be home till late. If you're hungry, there is tuna fish in the refrigerator. Make a sandwich. And there is cake in the cupboard. Love, Mother.*

Ten

*O*N *TUESDAY* the sun was playing hide-and-seek with the clouds, and a light breeze was teasing the trees when the Sunbirds met the Swifts on the Lyncook School Ball Park.

During infield practice, before play began, Bobby saw a left-hander warming up for the Swifts. He was Lefty Thorne, a kid with nothing but a straight ball and a slider. He didn't need anything else from what Bobby had heard through the grapevine.

"Hey, Fox! How many bases you going to steal today?"

The voice came from the third-base

bleachers. Bobby glanced there and saw the two long-haired kids. He wasn't surprised. They were his best fans.

"Got to get on base first," he said.

"Right!" the other agreed, grinning broadly.

In a few minutes the ump was shouting "Play ball!" and Bobby went up to the plate, his nerves jumping. He hated left-handed pitchers.

Lefty Thorne looked seven feet tall as he took his stretch, brought down his arms, then delivered. The ball seemed to come directly at Bobby, and he backed away from it.

"Strike!" said the ump.

Bobby looked at him, but the ump's attention was drawn to his counter, which he was holding in the palm of his left hand. It was, Bobby thought, a devious way of ignoring him.

Lefty rifled in another pitch for "Strike two!" and Bobby stepped out of the box. He took a deep breath, hoping that it would settle him down, and stepped back in again.

This time Lefty's pitch was outside, and so was the next. His fifth delivery came barreling in with something on it, because it started in toward Bobby, then headed out, like a snake that had seen something and wanted to get away from it.

Bobby swung. Bat met ball squarely and Bobby, dropping his bat, sped down the first-base line. The blow was a single over short, just six inches shy of being caught by Joe Morris, the Swifts' shortstop.

"There you are, Fox!" one of the kids yelled at him. "You're on!"

Bobby looked at third for a sign — any kind of sign — and got it. Play it safe, it said.

Eddie let the first pitch go by. It was a ball.

Bobby looked for the sign again. This time he got what he was hoping for — thumb to cap, to belt, to chest, and back to cap. The steal was on.

He waited for Lefty to get on the mound,

and took a lead. Remembering the pointers his father had given him, he made sure that his lead wasn't too big. Facing first base, a left-hander had a better advantage over the base runner than a right-hander did.

Lefty stretched, lowered his arms slowly, then quickly took his foot off the rubber and snapped the ball to first. Just as quickly Bobby shot back.

He was safe. But it was close.

The first baseman tossed the ball back to Lefty, and once again Bobby got ready. This time, as Lefty lowered his arms and started his pitch to the batter, Bobby was off like a shot.

He ran as hard as he could, but he felt as if his legs weren't really obeying his impulses. They didn't seem to be covering the ground as fast as he wanted them to.

He was within three feet of the bag when he saw the Swifts' second baseman reach for the ball and put it on him. By then he had slid in, a fraction of a second before the player had tagged him.

"Safe!" said the ump.

Bobby rose to his feet, not too happy about his run.

"Thataway to go, Fox!" yelled the two kids, almost in unison.

"Nice run, Fox!" another fan yelled.

Bobby winced. What had those crazy guys done? Tagged him with a nickname that might spread like measles?

With a one-and-one call on him, Eddie tied onto the next pitch and lofted it to center field, where it was easily put away for the first out.

Hank Spencer stepped to the plate and laid into the first pitch for a long foul strike. Coach Tarbell had shifted the lineup slightly, moving Hank up from seventh batter to third to take advantage of his long-ball hitting.

Lefty missed the plate on the next two pitches, then blazed one in that barely cut the inside corner. Two balls, two strikes.

Hank didn't appreciate the call. He stepped out of the box and looked out over the third-base bleachers for what might be a sign of sympathy from the fans. He got nothing but subtle chuckles and a sarcastic comment from a Swifts fan instead. "The plate's behind you, big shot."

Finding no sympathy, Hank returned to his position in the box and waited for Lefty's next pitch. It was a slider, and Hank laid into it. *Crack!* The ball shot out to left center for a clean hit. Bobby scored. By the time the ball was in, Hank was sliding into third.

"Hey, Fox!" exclaimed Andy Sanders, batting next. "You going for a base-stealing record or something?"

Bobby shrugged. "Something," he said, grinning. "Like runs."

He didn't mind the praise coming at him from the bench and the fans. It made him feel good, even though he wasn't thoroughly satisfied with himself. Well, at least, he had beaten the ball to the bag. That was the idea for a steal.

Andy Sanders grounded out, bringing up

Billy Trollop. Billy fouled a pitch to the backstop screen, then belted a line drive through second, scoring Hank. Snoop Myers couldn't find the handle of Lefty Thorne's pitches and went down swinging.

Sunbirds 2, Swifts 0.

B. J. Hendricks had it easy going with the Swifts' first two batters — a groundout to short, and a pop-up to Bobby.

Dick Flanders, the Swifts' left-handed left fielder, tied onto one for a sharp drive to center, only to get a single out of it. Then center fielder Tommy Elders poled an Empire Stater to Billy out in deep center, and that was it for the Swifts.

Jake Shakespeare, a utility outfielder, led off for the Sunbirds in the top of the second, and flied out to right. Neither Sherm nor B. J. was able to do any better, and the Swifts were back up to bat.

Butch Rollins, their burly catcher who sweated even when he wasn't doing anything, tagged B. J.'s first pitch for a two-bagger. Another double and a single followed, tying up the score.

Nuts, thought Bobby. *There goes our lead.*

A gangling redhead smashed a hot grounder down to third, snapping Bobby out of his doldrums. He scooped it up and whipped it underhand to second. Eddie caught it and snapped it to first. A fast double play.

Bobby pounded a fist proudly into the pocket of his glove. A play like that gave you a lift every time.

Lefty Thorne, socking a high bouncer back to B. J., ran only partway down to first as the Sunbirds' hurler caught the ball and tossed him out.

Bobby, leading off in the top of the third, waited out Lefty's pitches and earned a base on balls. Right off, Toody Goldstein, coaching at third, gave him the steal sign.

Taking a good lead, Bobby got set. He waited for Lefty to pass that limbo position, that point in his act when Bobby was sure that Lefty was going to throw either to first, or to home.

Standing on the mound like a tall mannequin with his arms and head moving in slow motion, Lefty glanced over his shoulder at Bobby. Then he looked back at the batter, quickly raised his leg, and started his delivery. Bobby took off.

About six feet from second base, as he saw the baseman nab the ball thrown to him by the catcher, Bobby slid. The baseman tagged him on the foot.

"You're out!" yelled the ump.

Bobby stared up at him, his heart pounding. But the man in blue had his face and forefinger pointed in another direction.

"Too bad, Fox!" one of the long-haired kids remarked as Bobby ran off the field.

"Can't win 'em all!" added the other.

More sympathetic remarks came from the guys on the bench. But sympathy wasn't what he needed, nor looked for. There was something he was not doing right. Perhaps he could have taken a bigger lead. Another foot might have made a difference. You can't be a Joe Morgan if you don't get the jump on the pitcher.

Bobby felt worse when Eddie tagged a pitch through an infield hole for a single. If he had been safe at second, he could have scored.

Hank poled a long fly to center that looked as if it were going over the fence. Instead, Tommy Elders, the Swifts' center fielder, got back in time, leaped and made a one-handed stabbing catch.

Then Andy started the ball rolling with a triple, followed by a walk by Billy, and a single by Snoop Myers. When the merry-go-round was over the Sunbirds had garnered two runs and were back in the lead.

Sunbirds 4, Swifts 2.

In the bottom of the third, B. J. held the Swifts down to a single and no runs. In the fourth, Sherm's single and B. J.'s walk looked as if another scoring inning were in the works. But Bobby flied out, Eddie grounded out, and Hank went down for his first strikeout.

The score was still unchanged as Bobby stepped to the plate in the top of the sixth. There was one out, B. J.'s pop-up to first.

Lefty breezed in a straight ball that was too good to be true. Bobby laid into it, smashing it hard down to third. Dropping his bat, he bolted for first, while out on the hot corner Steve Malloy missed the handle of the fast hop and let the ball streak through his legs.

Steve let his feelings go public by taking off his glove and throwing it against the ground, puffing up a cloud of dust.

As for Bobby, he'd take first base regardless of how he got it. Glancing toward third, he saw the steal sign coming at him again. Thanks, Snoop, he wanted to say. That's what I'm looking for.

This time he took a slightly extra lead and, as Lefty began his delivery, he took off.

He was there with time to spare.

"Hey, Fox! You did it, man!" someone shouted. It was one of his long-haired fans.

Eddie, a strike on him, let another pitch go by. "Ball!" cried the ump.

Bobby glanced at Snoop, and couldn't believe his eyes. Snoop was giving him the steal sign again! What? With one out? What was Coach Tarbell thinking of?

Well, so what? Stealing bases was his cup of tea. His *business*.

He took a long lead, got back quickly when Lefty tried to pick him off.

He resumed his position when Lefty got back on the mound, then took off like an Olympics hopeful as Lefty delivered.

Eddie let the pitch go by. The catcher caught it, whipped it hard to third, and the third baseman put it on Bobby.

"Out!" yelled the ump, loud enough for every person in the stands to hear him.

Bobby was sick. Rising gloomily to his feet, he trotted back to the dugout.

"Chin up," said the coach as Bobby

plunked himself down on the bench near him. "I wanted to see if you could do it. I figured, too, that if you got on third, an infield hit — no matter if it went through or not — would score you."

"Sorry it didn't work," said Bobby disappointedly.

"That's okay. Forget it."

Eddie flied out, ending the half inning.

The Swifts weren't able to bunch enough hits together during their next two trips to the plate, so lost to the Sunbirds 4–2.

After the hoopla was over — the Sunbirds praising the victory to each other — and the teams began to leave the field, Bobby heard his name called, and his heart soared to his throat. He'd recognize that voice anywhere.

"Dad!" he exclaimed as he saw his father coming toward him.

Someone was with him. A woman. She looked familiar.

Suddenly Bobby recalled where he had seen her before. It was at the ball park. She was the one who had driven up in a car, the one his father had gone to talk to.

There was a third person directly behind her.

Walter Wilson.

Eleven

*B*OBBY, *THIS* is Mrs. Wilson," said his father. "Mrs. Norma Wilson. And I guess you know Walter."

"Yes, I know him."

Bobby's eyes shifted to Walter, who was in his baseball uniform, and then to Mrs. Wilson. Embarrassment flushed his cheeks. Crazy thoughts rattled like rocks in his head. He didn't need it in writing to see that his father had found himself another woman. And that she was Walter's mother.

She put out her hand. He took it, reluctantly.

"Hello, Bobby. I'm glad to meet you. Your father has told me so much about you.

Walter must bring you over to our house sometime. We can have lunch together. Or even dinner. Would you like that?"

He shrugged. "I suppose so."

She had a slight build and brown hair, and wasn't bad-looking, much as he hated to admit it. Walter, whose hair and eyes resembled hers, seemed like a giant beside her.

Her fingers relaxed; their handshake, thank goodness, was over.

"We just got here," explained his father. "Saw the last half of the inning. Congratulations."

So he didn't see me running the bases, Bobby thought. *He didn't see me getting out sliding into third.*

"How did you guys make out?" he asked Walter in an attempt at conversation.

"We won."

"Who did you play?"

"The Swallows."

It was like dragging the answers out of him.

"How many hits did you get?" Walter suddenly asked him.

The question came as a surprise, and Bobby found himself staring at Walter.

"Two," he said.

"Pretty good."

Walter seemed tense, and met Bobby's eyes for only a moment at a time. *He's nervous,* thought Bobby. *Maybe he's going through the same kind of strain that I am, because we're living under similar conditions. Both of us have only a mother living with us.*

But I see my father once in a while. Walter never gets to see his. His father's dead.

"We better go," said Bobby's father. "See you again, Bobby."

"I must hurry home to make supper," murmured Mrs. Wilson, smiling jovially. "It was so nice to meet you, Bobby. And don't forget my invitation, will you?"

"No, I won't, Mrs. Wilson. It was nice meeting you, too."

He watched them leave. *That Walter,*

Bobby reflected. The kid certainly would never be known as a big talker.

He looked for Billy Trollop, found him, and rode home with him and his family.

After supper that night the doorbell rang. Bobby went to answer it. A woman stood there, a tall, pretty woman in a pink blouse and white slacks. She was carrying a cardboard box.

"Hello. I'm Mrs. Thorne," she said pleasantly. "Is your mother in?"

Almost automatically his eyes were drawn to the car at the curb. A white Charger.

A wisp of a smile curved his lips. So she was the one whom the car belonged to.

"Yes," he said, and, turning, called to his mother. "Mom! Someone here to see you!"

"Be right there!" replied his mother from another part of the house.

Bobby invited the woman in, and closed the door behind her. She wasn't smoking, but she could be carrying a pack of cigarettes in that huge white purse of hers. He took notice of her mouth, too. It was generously covered with lipstick, the same color that he had seen on one of the cigarette butts in the living room ashtray.

There was a hurried shuffling of sandals on the stairs, an overture announcing his mother's arrival. "Oh, hi, Jane," said Joyce Canfield, loose strands of hair dangling along the sides of her face. "You must forgive me. I'm cleaning, can you believe it? Seven-thirty in the evening, when most people are watching television, playing cards, or swimming in their pools, I'm cleaning!"

Mrs. Thorne smiled. "The woes of keeping house," she said.

"You said it!" said Bobby's mother, brushing back her hair. Her eyes fell upon the box Mrs. Thorne was carrying. "You have my order? So soon?"

"The cosmetics have already been manufactured, Joyce dear," said Mrs. Thorne sweetly. "All the company had to do was pack it and ship it."

"Fun-ny," replied Bobby's mother. She suddenly seemed to remember that Bobby was there, and officially introduced him. Bobby and Mrs. Thorne shook hands.

"He's a handsome boy, Joyce. And about the age of my own son. How old are you, Bobby?"

"Twelve."

"My David's thirteen. You should know him. He pitches for the Swifts."

"Oh! You mean Lefty? Sure, I know Lefty. Everybody does. We beat his team today."

"Don't I know it," she said. "He's been moping around the house ever since he came home from the game."

Bobby's mother invited her into the living room where they sat down, lit up cigarettes, and chatted. That's what they had been doing the day he had come home and found the cigarette butts in the ashtray, he thought.

He excused himself, went to the den, and turned on the TV, just in time to watch a final chase scene on his favorite detective show. The hero captured his man, subtly accepted the accolades from his superior, and the case was closed.

It was shortly after lunch the next day when someone rang the doorbell. Bobby answered it. It was Billy Trollop.

"Hi, Billy," he greeted, somewhat surprised. It wasn't often that Billy came over to see him anymore. "What's new?"

Billy's visits used to be as regular as clockwork, but ever since the divorce of Bobby's parents they had dropped to almost nil. Bobby supposed that Billy was embarrassed to come anymore. But he wasn't sure and he didn't ask.

"There's a guy down on your beach wants to see you," said Billy.

"Who?"

"Walter Wilson."

"Walter Wilson?" Bobby's eyebrows arched. "What does he want?"

He had no idea where Walter lived, except that the burly pitcher for the Cowbirds didn't live in *this* neck of the woods.

"I think he'd like a ride in your boat," said Billy.

"What?" Bobby frowned. *Walter walked all the way here for a ride in my boat?* he thought.

He remembered yesterday's meeting with Walter and his mother. That brief meeting showed him that Walter was in the same boat that he was. Maybe Walter was in one that was even worse. He didn't have a father, and that must have hurt him. But, being a tough kid he didn't want anyone to know how he really felt. Maybe he needed someone to talk it over with.

I think I know how he feels, Bobby thought. *Since my parents have divorced I have felt awfully alone. Why is it? Is it that because when we're hurt we're afraid to open up and maybe be hurt more?*

"Well, what shall I tell him?" asked Billy.

"I'll talk with him," said Bobby.

They walked down to the beach, and Bobby saw Walter standing on the dock by the hoist, looking at the interior of the boat.

"Hi, Walter," greeted Bobby.

"Hi," said Walter. "How are you doing?"

"Okay."

"I came over to take a ride in your boat," said Walter. He held Bobby's eyes for a few seconds, then bent over, picked up a flat stone and launched it out over the lake. The stone hit the water, skipped half a dozen times, then disappeared.

"I don't know whether I should," Bobby said.

Walter peered at him. "Why not? Your father said it's all right. That's why I came. He said that you wouldn't mind taking me out for a ride."

Bobby looked at him. "My father said that?"

"Of course. Look, do you think I'd walk all the way over here if he hadn't asked me to? He said to phone you first, but I didn't think it was necessary. I figured that you'd be somewhere around here, anyway." He launched another stone across the surface of the lake and watched it skip. "I walked about two miles to get here. You want me to walk back without a ride?"

Bobby thought a minute. "Wait here," he said finally. "I'll get the key."

Twelve

*B*OBBY GOT the key from the house and returned to the dock. He released the catch that secured the iron wheel, then lowered the boat into the water.

"Okay. Get in," he said to Walter.

Walter got in.

"Don't you want to come along?" Bobby called to Billy.

"No, thanks," said Billy.

Bobby shrugged and inserted the key into the ignition, started the engine, and backed the boat slowly out into deeper water. Then he turned the wheel and cautioned Walter, who was crouched against the gunwale behind him, to hang on. Then he thrust the throttle forward. The boat lurched ahead, bow rising, engine roaring. After a few moments the bow settled down, and the boat bounced over the choppy water.

A sailboat was in his path, tacking toward the east shore of the lake, and Bobby turned the wheel slightly to avoid running into it. As he headed toward the north end of the lake, he began to wonder why Walter really had come over. Maybe he wanted to talk about their parents. Bobby didn't know if he wanted to do that. He hardly knew Walter well enough to judge his sincerity.

He glanced over his shoulder to see what Walter was doing, and almost jumped out of his skin as he saw the boy trying to light up a cigarette.

"No smoking, Walt!" he shouted.

At that same instant the blazing match that Walter was holding to the tip of his cigarette went out. Ignoring Bobby's warning, he tore another match from the book, and struck it. Again it went out.

This time he knelt down. And, with the protection of the windshield, he started to strike another match.

Mounting anger, mixed with an equal proportion of fear, surged through Bobby. "Walt! Did you hear me? No smoking, I said!"

As the second warning left his lips, he saw Walter flick the cigarette over his shoulder. His intention was for it to go overboard. It didn't. The wind took it and swept it back into the boat, into the engine compartment, where it seemed to die out for a moment, but blazed back to life.

"Get that cigarette!" Bobby started to yell. But just then the red tip of the cigarette touched the leaky gas line and ignited it.

The explosion that followed was loud, shattering, bomblike. Bobby saw the blinding flash of fire, then was knocked against the instrument panel and the wheel. Dazed and scared half to death, he turned and saw Walter lying on the deck, flung there by the explosion.

Remembering that the gas tank was underneath the forward deck, his fear increased a hundredfold. Rushing to Walter and grabbing him by the shoulders, he yelled shrilly, "Get up and jump out! Quick, before the gas tank explodes, too!"

They jumped out, and began swimming as fast as they could away from the boat. A moment later the gas tank did exactly what Bobby had said it would. It exploded, blowing a gaping hole through the bow, and sending flames billowing madly into the air. Rocked by the terrific blast, the boat heaved. Its bow ripped apart, fragments of it flying all over, some within only a few feet of the boys.

When the sound of the explosion died away, Bobby paused and looked back. Deep anguish overwhelmed him as he saw only a cloud of dark gray smoke rising slowly upward from the spot where the boat had sunk to its watery grave.

The boat had been a pride of his father's. Roger Canfield had left it at home only because Bobby had liked it so much, too.

Suddenly it occurred to him how close he must have been to death, and he shuddered. He thought of Walter, and fear gripped him as he wondered if Walter had been struck by the flying pieces of the boat.

He looked around anxiously, and relief came over him as he saw Walter about ten feet away, looking back at the grim pall of smoke and the floating debris.

"You all right?" Bobby asked.

"Yeah. How about you?" replied Walter.

"I'm okay."

Walter glanced toward shore. "That's a long way to swim," he observed.

"Wait a minute," said Bobby. "There should be some life jackets floating around."

They both looked around for the life jackets.

"There's one!" Walter shouted suddenly. "And there's another!"

Bobby saw the two life jackets that Walter was pointing to. Brushing aside the thought of the lost boat, he started to swim to one of them, while Walter swam to the other. They put the life jackets over their heads, buckled them, and tightened up the belts in front.

Seconds later a new sound reached Bobby's ears. It grew louder and louder. Looking about him, he saw a power boat speeding toward them. Two others were heading toward them from other directions.

"Looks like we won't have to swim it!" exclaimed Walter, smiling with relief.

"Right!" replied Bobby, feeling light and buoyant as the life jacket kept him afloat.

The nearest boat slowed down as it approached. There were two people in it, a man and a woman.

"Oh, wow!" yelled the woman, who looked to be in her early twenties. "I can't believe it! They're alive!"

Her eyes were wide as she stared at the two boys. Both she and the man were wearing swimsuits.

"Pull up beside him first," said the man, pointing toward Walter.

The woman, handling the steering wheel, drew up beside Walter, and the man proceeded to haul the boy into the boat. Then he hauled in Bobby.

"Anybody else besides you two in that boat?" the man inquired.

"No. It was just us," puffed Bobby, the water dripping off him.

"We heard the explosion and saw the fire. How could a boat explode? You boys were real lucky."

"I know," said Bobby, glancing at Walter. Would Walter tell, he wondered, what caused the explosion?

But Walter remained silent. He was sitting on one of the seats, his hair matted to his head, his clothes stuck to his skin, his attention drawn to the shore toward which they were heading.

"What happened?" the woman asked.

There was the inevitable question. And again Bobby waited for Walter to say something. But he didn't. He was ignoring them completely.

"I don't know," said Bobby. "The engine blew. We jumped out of the boat, then the gas tank blew."

I can't squeal on Walter, thought Bobby. *It's up to him to tell them how careless he's been.*

The man and woman exchanged a look.

"Where do you boys live?" the man asked.

"I live near the lake. Over there," said Bobby, pointing to the beach house that was easily visible.

"And you?" the man asked Walter.

"I live on Maple Avenue," said Walter.

The girl turned the wheel and headed the boat toward the beach house.

The man looked over Bobby's arms, legs, and body for bruises.

"I'm okay," Bobby assured him.

"I just want to check," replied the man.

He gave Walter a close looking-over too, then said, "I guess you're both all right." He sat back and relaxed, relieved that the boys weren't injured.

When they arrived on shore Bobby's mother was there waiting for them.

Thirteen

I *JUST KNEW* it was our boat!" cried
Bobby's mother, hugging Bobby fiercely.
"When I heard that explosion and then saw
the boat was gone from the hoist — I just
knew it!"

Bobby and Walter had removed their life
jackets and had left them on the deck. The
rescuers were leaving.

"You could have been killed!" his mother
went on. "You know that? You could have
been killed!"

Bobby didn't answer. He stood there,
shivering, waiting for his mother to get hold
of herself.

"What I would like to know," she said, staring directly at him, "is why you took the boat without permission. Explain *that* to me."

She was trembling, and her eyes were red from crying.

"I gave Walter a ride," Bobby answered. "I mean, that's why I—"

She looked at Walter, and frowned. "Walter? Walter who?"

"Walter Wilson."

"I don't think I've seen you before," she said, her voice softer now. "Where do you live, Walter?"

Walter looked at her. "On Maple Avenue," he answered calmly.

"Maple Avenue?" She stared at him. "That's about two miles from here. Do you play on Bobby's team? Is that why you're here?"

"No, ma'am."

"You just came to take a ride in the boat?"

"Yes, ma'am."

Bobby's mother glanced at Bobby, her

eyes probing. "I never heard you talk of him. Is he a new friend of yours?"

"No. He's . . ." Bobby couldn't get the words out.

"He's what?" his mother said, trying to wring the rest of the sentence out of him.

"You won't like to hear this, Mom," he said.

"I'm going to hear it sometime," she said. "You might as well tell it to me now."

He got up his gumption and formed the words in his mind first before uttering them. "He's the son of the woman Dad has been seeing lately," he said.

"Oh?" Her eyes widened, her cheeks flushed as she glanced back at Walter. "And because of that you felt that you should give him a ride in the boat? Is that it?"

"No, Mom. It wasn't like that at all. Walter told me that Dad had said it was okay." He paused, shivering, as he watched his mother staring at Walter Wilson. "I'm cold, Mom," he said. "I'd like to get out of these wet clothes."

She didn't answer him right away. She seemed too preoccupied with unpleasant thoughts.

"Come on," she said finally, drawing him toward the steps. "You, too, Walter. I'll drive you home."

"Crazy!" Roger Canfield shouted. "Crazy! Crazy! You're lucky you're alive, you know that? You and Walter both! Oh — wow!"

He had come over to the house as soon as he had heard from Walter about the boat's sinking. He had been at Walter's mother's house at the time, had heard Walter's version of the explosion and the sinking, and was here now to hear Bobby's.

He stood before Bobby, his chest heaving, his face wet with perspiration.

"One thing I want to get straight," he said firmly. "Walter told me that you were smoking a cigarette. That when you tossed it overboard, the wind blew it against the engine."

"He lied!" Bobby cried. "He's the one who

141

lighted a cigarette. He threw it away when I told him not to smoke.

"He told me he doesn't smoke," said Roger, looking deep into Bobby's eyes.

"The heck he doesn't! Dad, you know I don't smoke! I've never smoked a cigarette in my life!"

"That's true," said Bobby's mother. "If he had, I would have known about it."

Roger Canfield sighed. He was more composed now, his wits collected. "I believe you, Bobby. You've always been honest with your mother and me. Okay, that's all I want to know." He looked at his ex-wife. "There's a good insurance policy on that boat. You should get almost enough from it to buy another one, if you want to."

"I'll get the insurance money," she replied, gazing at him from behind amber sunglasses. "But I'll have to think about getting another boat. After what happened, I'm not sure I will. Anyway, I've already thought about it. I think it's only fair that you should have half of it."

"No. I don't need it," he said. "You can have all of it. That's not important to me."

"You sure?"

"I'm sure. I want to say, too, that it wasn't Bobby's fault that the boat blew up. I should have had that leaky line repaired a long time ago. I'm to blame for it." He paused. "Just the same, I've got a thing or two to say to that Walter." He turned to Bobby. "How come you gave him a ride in the boat in the first place?"

"Because he asked me to. He said that you told him it was all right for me to give him a ride."

Roger's mouth pursed. "I didn't tell him that at all. I guess I'll have to speak to him about that."

"Dad, I think that Walter is a pretty lonely kid who's looking for a friend or something," said Bobby. "Every time he says or does something, he's awkward about it. The more I'm near him, the more I've noticed it."

Roger frowned. "I've wondered about

143

that, Bobby," he said. He was quiet a moment or two, then he cleared his throat. "Well, I'll go now. Unless something happens, I'll see you on Saturday morning. Good-bye, Joyce."

"Good-bye, Roger."

He put on his yellow cap and walked out. Bobby walked out with him. "Dad," he said, thoughtfully, "whatever happened to Walter's father?"

"He got killed a couple of years ago in an automobile accident. Why?"

Bobby shrugged. "Just wondered."

Not until his father had entered his car and driven off did Bobby go back into the house and close the door.

He wasn't ripe for the game against the Swallows. He didn't feel like playing baseball any more than he felt like flying to the moon. And it wasn't the bruises that made him feel like that. What few there were wouldn't slow him up a bit.

It was the loss of the boat, and the almost

certain fact that his mother would not purchase another one to take its place.

Somehow, even though he hadn't used it much, the boat had been the one tangible thread that kept him close to his father during the weekdays. The weekends took care of themselves. The two were together then.

Nevertheless, he went to the game. He felt he had an obligation. Billy Trollop's father picked him up as usual in his big sedan.

The Sunbirds were up first and Bobby stepped to the plate, the bat feeling as if it weighed a ton. Red Burke, a tall right-hander with red, bushy eyebrows, was pitching for the Swallows. He had trouble finding the plate with his first three throws, and just like that the count was three and nothing.

Bobby stood at the plate, leaving the bat on his shoulder.

Red came back and placed his next two pitches directly over the heart of the plate, and then it was three and two.

Bobby stepped out of the box and killed a little time by rubbing his sweaty palms against his pants, and then rubbing the thin handle of his bat between his legs. The act wasn't only to dry the palms and the handle of the bat. It also provided a few seconds for some strong concentration.

But the few seconds didn't help Bobby. Red Burke breezed the next one in, just cutting the inside corner, and Bobby swung and missed.

He went back to the bench, embarrassed. It was the first time he had struck out while leading off.

"You can't steal bases if you don't get on, Fox," said Sherm, smiling at him.

"Glad you told me that," said Bobby.

Hank Spencer got the only hit during that half inning, a single through short.

B. J. Hendricks threw enough pitches to get out six men before he was able to vanquish the necessary three. And without allowing a run, at that.

In the top of the second inning Snoop

146

Myers, the utility infielder, singled after Billy Trollop had flied out, and Jake Shakespeare walked. Then Sherm was given a free ticket, too, loading the bases.

"Let's send up a designated hitter," said Eddie.

"Yeah, why don't we?" replied Hank enthusiastically.

"Because we don't have one, for one thing," said Bobby, who had gotten over most of his strikeout pain. "For another thing, it ain't in the rules."

Red Burke rifled in two strike pitches, and was about to go for his possible third, when B. J. stepped out of the box. The ump called time.

"Three men on, B. J.!" yelled Eddie. "Knock 'em in!"

B. J. stepped back into the box, bold, courageous, eager, and slammed a hot grounder to short. It was one of the quickest double plays in the league's history. Three outs.

The Swallows came up and began where

they had left off, banging out three hits in a row, including a long triple by their long-ball hitter, Tom Bootree. Two runs crossed the plate.

Top of the third. Bobby led off again, fouling the first two pitches, then forcing Red to throw four more before getting his well-earned walk.

On first base he looked for a sign from the third-base coach. *Play it safe.* He did, while Eddie took a strike call.

Then he got the sign he had somehow expected, even with the Sunbirds trailing by two runs. *Steal.*

He beat the throw by a mile.

"Thataway, Fox!" yelled a fan as Bobby stood on the bag, his hands on his hips.

Eddie flied out to right on the next pitch. Bobby, tagging up, had no trouble making it to third.

Hank reached out after an outside pitch and laid it over first base, bringing in Bobby. Then Andy tripled, scoring Hank. But that

was it as Billy and Snoop got out on a pop-up and a grounder, respectively.

"Your father must have been pretty sore when he heard about the boat," said Billy, as he sat next to Bobby on the bench.

"Don't think he wasn't," said Bobby. "On top of the accident, Walter told him that *I* was the cause of the fire. That *I* lit the cigarette."

"Wow. Your father didn't believe that bull, did he?"

"Not really. That was why he came over to talk with me about it. Anyway, I don't think it's all Walter's fault, and I told my father that."

Billy looked at him. "What do you mean?"

"Do you know that Walter's father is dead? That he was killed in an accident?"

"No."

"Well, he was," said Bobby. "I think that has a lot to do with the way Walter behaves. He tries to pretend he's cool, except that he makes a fool of himself and doesn't know it."

Suddenly the thought occurred to him: *Have I been acting that way, too? Oh, man!*

The Swallows picked up one run during their turn at bat. But the Sunbirds came through for two more in the top of the fourth, during which Bobby chalked up his second stolen base of the game after belting out a liner over the second-base bag.

Horse collars went up on the scoreboard until the bottom of the fifth when the Swallows drove in two runs, then held the Sunbirds scoreless the last two innings.

It was 5–4, in the Swallows' favor, when the game ended.

Fourteen

ROGER CANFIELD arrived at ten minutes of nine Saturday morning, picked up Bobby, and drove to Meadow Park.

"I see that they're calling you the Fox," he said as they drove slowly and quietly through the streets of Lyncook. "That's quite a tag."

"You wouldn't believe who stuck it on me," exclaimed Bobby.

"Oh, yes, I would," replied his father, chuckling. "I was there when those two kids watching you practice base stealing called you Fox. Remember?"

152

"Oh, that's right," said Bobby, now recalling the day vividly. "I remember." He laughed. "I can think of worse names than that!"

"Right. The only thing about Fox is, you'll have to keep working hard to live up to it. And I think you will. You're doing fine."

Bobby looked at his father. "Were you at the game Thursday, Dad?"

"No. I'm not always free in the afternoons. I read about you in last night's paper. There wasn't much, but it's usually the winning team that gets most of the publicity, anyway."

Not always free in the afternoons? Where was he? Visiting Mrs. Wilson?

No sooner had the thought popped into Bobby's mind than he felt ashamed of himself. He shouldn't have thought that of his father. What his father did was his business. Anyway, what was so bad about his visiting Mrs. Wilson? He was divorced. And she was a widow.

Darn! he thought. *What am I doing? Getting on my father because I love him so? Should I close my eyes to all the things he does, and open them only when I'm with him? Doing things with him? What is the right thing to do?*

He didn't know. But deep in his heart he wished that his father would not see another woman. Not ever.

They reached the park. Roger Canfield parked the car and locked it, taking no chance even though the car was six years old.

They got out and walked toward the picnic pavilion, beyond which was the sandy beach. For a while they talked about baseball, and Bobby's growing experience as a hitter and a base stealer. Being both was extraordinary, according to his father, for all good hitters were not base stealers. Dave Kingman, Mike Schmidt, Greg Luzinski, a few of the names that rolled off his tongue, were good with the stick, but once on base — unless they drove the ball out of the park — they usually left it up to the next batters to move them along.

Base stealing was an extra talent inherent in one whose body had a natural development for speed and coordination. It wasn't everyone who was blessed with those physical attributes. Bobby had them. All he had to do was to keep working on them, and not to let them get dormant. Roger Canfield talked as if he enjoyed saying what he was saying. He knew baseball from top to bottom and sideways, having played in the minors for five years after graduating from high school.

Somehow Bobby had the feeling that his father was sorry he had quit at so early an age, but his father had never said so.

They found an empty bench on the beach and sat down. Neither said a word for several minutes. They just watched the waves lapping up on shore, people swimming, and sailboats leaning against the wind.

Then his father said something that gave

Bobby a start. Not sure he had heard right, Bobby looked closely at his father. "What did you say, Dad?"

"I said that I'm taking a job on a freighter," repeated Roger Canfield. "I've always wanted to take a trip around the world. This time I'm going to do it."

Bobby stared at him. The thought that he wouldn't see his father for many months frightened him to the bone. "You're going to quit your job?"

"I'll have to."

For a long minute Bobby was silent. "How — how long will you be gone, Dad?" he asked finally.

"Could be a year. It depends. If I like it, I might stay with it."

Bobby felt an ache in his throat. He hated to ask the next question, but he had to. "You going to take anybody with you, Dad?"

"No. I'm going alone."

That meant he wouldn't be taking Mrs. Wilson. He had no intention of marrying her, then. That thought made Bobby feel slightly better, anyway.

"Can I go with you?"

The question was crazy to ask. He knew that, but there was always that one-in-a-million chance that the answer would be "yes."

"You know you can't, Bobby," said his father, pricking his son's dream balloon. "It's just impossible. No, I'm going alone. I'll miss you very much, but I've got to get away from here for a while. It's — it's hard to explain."

"That's okay, Dad. You don't have to explain."

Restless, that was the word in a nutshell. His mother had mentioned it dozens of times. Roger Canfield was the most restless man on earth. He couldn't stay put in one place for any length of time. He couldn't hold onto a job for any length of time. There was something in his blood, she said, that egged him on to other places, to do other things. That she had lived with him as long as she had was a miracle.

"I got the truth out of Walter about that smoking business," his father said, changing the subject. "He admitted he had lied."

Bobby met his father's eyes. "I bet he had a tough time admitting it."

"Yes, he did."

"You won't ever marry Mrs. Wilson, will you, Dad?" said Bobby earnestly.

His father's eyes shone. "No. And that's a promise. As a matter of fact, I've stopped seeing her." He paused. "Talking about the Wilsons, when is your team going to play Walter's again? I don't want to miss it."

"I'm not sure. Maybe next week."

"Okay. I'll keep my eye on the papers."

At Municipal Park that afternoon they watched the Lyncook Giants beat the Valley Bobcats. The next day Roger Canfield borrowed a 12-foot boat from a friend of his, and, using fishpoles that he still kept in the beach house, spent the whole day fishing with his son. It was, Bobby thought, like having a good-bye supper with his father.

He had a so-so day against the Redlegs on Tuesday, getting one walk and no hits. But he had one stolen base, and the Sunbirds had taken the game, 8–6.

It was on Thursday that they played the Cowbirds. A big crowd attended. Among them were the two long-haired fans whose names Bobby still did not know.

"Hi ya, Fox. How you doin'?" one of them asked, grinning.

"Okay," he said. "How about you?"

"Just great," came the response.

His father was among the first to come, as if to make sure of his seat near the third-base sack. He smiled and waved, saying a lot just in those silent gestures.

His father's words rang again in Bobby's ears, tolling in the back of his mind. *I've always wanted to take a trip around the world. This time I'm going to do it.* He tried to concentrate on the game. How could he play a good game of baseball if he kept thinking all the time of his father and what his father was going to do?

Grandpa Alex was there, too, wearing a hat to cover his bald head, and dark glasses to shield his eyes from the glaring sun.

The sight of them warmed Bobby's heart. Next to his father, Grandpa Alex was the greatest living man on earth.

The Sunbirds had first bats.

"Look who's on the mound," Billy said as Bobby started swinging two bats, each with a metal doughnut around the fat part.

"I see," observed Bobby, who hadn't thought much about it. He had other — more important — thoughts on his mind.

"Play ball!" the umpire announced.

The crowd cheered and clapped.

"Get a hit, Bobby! Get on, kid!" a fan yelled.

"Come on, Fox! Start it off!" another fan chimed in.

Bobby tossed aside one of the bats, removed the doughnut from the one he kept, and stepped to the plate. He dug into the dirt for secure footing, then held up his bat and looked across the short span between home and the mound at Walter Wilson.

Walter looked big, strong, and menacing. He looked as if he could throw a ball two hundred miles an hour, and was going to do it with every pitch.

He stepped on the rubber, stretched, and delivered. The ball streaked in, knee-high and a hair inside. Bobby heard it explode in the catcher's mitt.

"Strike!" boomed the ump.

Bobby looked back at him in surprise. The ump, busy adjusting his counter, ignored him.

Another pitch.

"Strike two!"

Bobby stepped out of the box. He wasn't happy about that call, either.

"Come on, Fox!" yelled one of the long-haired fans. "You can't steal a base if you don't get on!"

He stepped back into the box. Then

Walter proceeded to fire four more pitches, all balls.

Bobby walked.

He looked for the sign from the third-base coach. *Play it safe.*

Eddie took a called strike.

Then it came — thumb to cap, to belt, to chest, and back to cap. The steal was on.

Fifteen

*B*OBBY LOOKED up at the crowd and saw his father and grandfather. Both were watching him intently, waiting to see if he would run. Grandpa Alex then leaned over and said something to Bobby's father.

Bobby reverted his attention to Walter, who was getting set to pitch.

I wonder if seeing me will make him think about that boat accident, thought Bobby. *I wonder if he feels sorry at all that he had lied to my father.*

Bobby took his lead.

I've got to make this one good, he promised himself, forgetting Walter and his connection with the boat accident for a minute. *I've got to show Dad that all that training paid off.*

Walter stretched, brought down his arms. Then, like a shot, he fired the ball to first.

The throw could not have been more accurate, nor quicker. The first baseman caught the ball near the bag and tagged Bobby on the leg just a fraction of a second before he could get back.

"Ouuuut!" shouted the ump.

Bobby trotted to the Sunbirds' bench, his head bowed in embarrassment, as hooplas exploded from the Cowbirds' fans.

Sympathetic remarks came from the two long-haired kids. "That's okay, Fox. Don't let it get you down. You'll be up again."

They were okay guys. At a time like this he could use all the moral support he could get.

But he had let his father and grandfather down. That's what bothered him.

Eddie smashed a single to left, only to perish on first as both Hank and Andy failed to connect with safeties.

B. J., pitching for the Sunbirds, gave up a hit and a walk as the Cowbirds came to bat. But that was all.

Billy, leading off in the top of the second, connected with a high fly that might have landed in the middle of the lake, if it had traveled horizontally. As it was, Nick Tully, the Cowbirds' shortstop, caught it just outside of the base path.

Walter rifled in two pitches to Snoop Myers. Both were balls.

Then he accidentally laid one in where Snoop must have seen it hanging like a balloon. Swinging with all his might, Snoop met the ball right at its equator and sent it out of the park.

Cheers exploded from the fans as Snoop circled the bases. Even the Cowbirds' fans gave him an ovation. Snoop took off his cap and politely bowed.

The next two batters, Toody and Sherm, went down without a hit.

Again the Cowbirds, and again the Sunbirds, breezed through their turns at bat without scoring a run. Walter had made a threat by driving out a long double, but good defense on the part of Eddie and Snoop had kept him from going any farther than second base.

The big blast happened in the bottom of the third. It started with B. J. walking Jake Hollister, who went to third on a sharp two-bagger by Larry Jones. Then Adam Hooton singled, scoring Jake.

Bobby called time and trotted to the mound, thinking that B. J. needed a few minutes' rest to get himself back in order. Andy, Eddie, and Snoop joined the huddle.

"Take it easy, B. J.," said Bobby. "You're working too fast."

"Keep 'em low," suggested Andy.

"Just get 'em out," offered Snoop.

The three infielders returned to their positions, leaving B. J. alone with his problem. Nick Tully swung at B. J.'s first pitch, a long fly ball to left field. Hank put it away with ease.

"Thataway to go, old fella!" exclaimed Bobby.

Up came Foster Moore, the Cowbirds' burly center fielder, waving his bat over his head like a war club. Everybody backed up, knowing Foster's power.

Bang! He sliced a single over short, and Larry scored.

Walter came up again, keeping the Sunbirds playing deep. Batting seventh meant that he was one of those rare birds, a hitting pitcher.

He proved it again on the third pitch. The blow looked as if it might be a home run as the ball soared to deep center field. But it struck the fence and bounced back, and Walter finished up on third. A run had scored on the hit, and the Cowbirds went out in front, 4–1.

I don't know why I should feel sorry for him, thought Bobby. *He hits like a fool on the ball field.*

Second baseman Ed Michaels kept up the hitting barrage with a run-driving-in single, and Bobby began to wonder just how long this merry-go-round would last. There was still only one out, and the Cowbirds were hitting the old apple as if they couldn't get out if they tried.

Butch Mortz, the last man on the totem pole for the Cowbirds, then slashed a hot grounder to Bobby. Bobby caught it on a hop, fired the ball to second, and Eddie relayed it to first. A double play!

"Oh, wow," murmured Bobby under his breath as he trotted off the field. "It's about time."

"Maybe you ought to take me out, Coach," said B. J., slump-shouldered as he sat back against the dugout wall. "They're making mincemeat out of me."

Coach Tarbell looked at him. "I want you to pitch this game, B. J. Ollie's only had one day's rest. Take your time out there. Don't rush it, and you'll come through A-okay. All right?"

B. J. shrugged. "You're the boss, Coach," he said.

Leading off, Snoop Myers again surprised everyone by banging out a safe hit, even though it was only a single. Toody walked, and Sherm socked the first pitch for a streaking double between left and center fields. Snoop and Toody scored.

B. J., whom no one expected to hit safely, didn't. However, he managed to get on, thanks to an error by Nick Tully, the Cowbirds' shortstop.

With runners on first and second, Bobby was up again. He thought of his father and grandfather sitting in the stands, watching him, waiting to see what he would do. He remembered what had happened to him during that first inning when he had tried to steal. He had certainly flubbed badly then.

What was he going to show them now?

He looked at Walter, and waited for the pitch he wanted. He got it after three pitches, an over-the-heart-of-the-plate fastball.

But the blow was just a solid smash down to short, and Nick threw him out.

Well, at least he had hit the ball. That was a consolation.

Eddie came through with a single, driving in Sherm. The run brought the Sunbirds up to within one score of the Cowbirds, 5–4. The Sunbirds were back in the ball game.

Then Hank hit into a double play, and the top of the fourth inning was over.

Only Larry Jones managed to get on base as the Cowbirds took their turns at the plate. He died on first, however.

In the top of the fifth, Billy got a single and advanced to second on Nick's groundball error, a grass-streaker hit by Toody. But they perished on the bases, too.

B. J. mowed down Ed Michaels with a strikeout, then got support from Billy as the center fielder hauled in Butch Mortz's cloud-scraping fly. Jake Hollister made the third out.

"Okay, B. J.," said Snoop as the left-hander headed for the plate. "Start it off. I guarantee something's going to happen."

B. J. obliged by dropping a single over first. Then Bobby, his fourth time at bat, came up with his first hit. *It's about time,* he thought.

He didn't look for his father and grand-father now. He didn't have to. Part of that applause he heard must be theirs.

But suddenly, he remembered that his father would be gone soon. And an ache lodged in his throat.

Change your mind, Dad, he pleaded. *Please change your mind.*

Neither Eddie nor Hank was able to hit balls where they weren't. But Andy came through with a smashing drive over short, scoring B. J. to tie up the ball game, 5–5.

The Sunbirds' bench went wild. The fans

went crazy. You would have thought it was Shea Stadium with the Mets coming from behind to tie it up with the Phillies.

Billy kept the game rolling with a walk. Then Snoop smashed one through the shortstop's legs, scoring Bobby and putting the Sunbirds ahead, 6–5. Toody grounded out.

"We're in! We're in!" Snoop shouted wildly as he came running in for his glove.

"The ball game isn't over yet," reminded Walter, heading for his bench.

He was right. In the Cowbirds' half of the inning a single by Ted Lacey, then a triple off the big bat of Jake Hollister knotted the score again, 6–6.

The moments got hairier when the Sunbirds came up as Bobby, third man in the batting order, watched Sherm go to the plate and fly out. Next up was B. J., who made it two outs by grounding out to first.

"Take the last one, Walt!" shouted Butch Mortz, the Cowbirds' catcher, as Bobby stepped into the batting box.

Bobby ignored him. He dug his toes into the dirt and waited for Walter to come to him.

Walter did, on the second pitch. Bobby drove it over second base, a clean single.

He couldn't believe it. He needed that hit. The team needed it.

He glanced over to the third-base coaching box. The steal sign was on!

He took his lead, careful this time not to go too far. Walter got set, then snapped the ball to first.

Bobby scooted back in time.

Keep throwing them over here, Walter, he wanted to say. One bad throw and I'm gone.

As it was, he didn't have to wait for a bad throw. He went down on the pitch, and made it by a mile.

He could hear his father's and grandfather's cheers. And he looked at the crowd and saw them standing up together, clapping like crazy. His heart tingled.

Again he sized up the situation. There was no steal sign being offered him by the third-base coach. But would that mastermind on the mound, Walter Wilson, expect him to steal third with two outs?

Walter got set to pitch, and Bobby got set to run. On the pitch, Bobby took off. Eddie's swing and miss helped, for the catcher failed to get the ball to third on time, and Bobby was safe.

"Hey, Fox!" yelled one of his long-haired fans enthusiastically. "You made it, man!"

"Steal home, Fox!" shouted the other half of the pair.

Steal home? No way!

But — why not? *Why not?* Who would expect him to steal home with two outs? Maybe those two long-haired fans of his. But who else?

The more he considered the idea, the better it sounded.

He sized up the situation. There was a fifty-fifty chance of Eddie's getting a safe hit.

Maybe less. His failure to hit would mean that the Cowbirds, taking their last bats, would have three outs to make in their attempt to break the tie.

I'll have to try it, decided Bobby. *It makes sense.* Thanks, kid! he wanted to yell to the long-haired fan who had suggested the idea.

He took a lead, standing straight so that Walter would not get any silly thoughts about him. That he catch Walter — and Butch — off guard was of utmost importance.

Walter stretched, glanced briefly at Bobby, then started his delivery. At the same time, Bobby started to dash for home.

Running as fast as he could go, he was within a few yards of home when he saw the ball strike Butch's mitt. There was only one thing he could do now, and he did it. He hit the dirt. Sliding across the plate, he saw Butch falling over it toward him.

Butch put the ball on him. But the call that boomed from the umpire told the story.

"Safe!"

"Thataboy, Fox!" yelled his long-haired fans. "You did it, man! You did it!"

From the stands came the booming cheers of the other Sunbirds fans. Bobby's father and grandfather joined in the cheering. It was the happiest moment of his life.

The half inning ended as Eddie flied out.

Adam led off at the bottom of the seventh with a single. Nick flied out, then Foster hit into a double play, and it was over; 7–6, in favor of the Sunbirds.

Bobby's father and grandfather came off the stands. But they had to wait for the mob that surrounded their hero to disperse before they could get to him.

"So they call you the Fox, do they?" exclaimed Grandpa Alex, his eyes twinkling with admiration. "Well, you certainly deserve it. Guess all that practice that your father and I put you through helped, didn't it?"

"It sure did, Grandpa!" replied Bobby happily.

His father beamed with pride. "Man, you can *run*," he said. "And don't let anybody tell you different!"

Bobby smiled. "Thanks, Dad." He paused, his mind suddenly shifting to another, more personal, matter. "Dad, are you still going?"

"On that freighter job? Yes, Bobby, I am. But, don't worry. I'll be back. And who knows? Probably by then things might change. You can never tell."

"No, Dad," said Bobby. "I guess you can't."

Maybe it is best this way, thought Bobby.

It was a good feeling to know for certain that his father would be coming back, and, who knew, by that time he might just be the best base stealer in the state.

How many of these Matt Christopher sports classics have you read?

Baseball

❏ Baseball Pals
❏ Catcher with a Glass Arm
❏ Challenge at Second Base
❏ The Diamond Champs
❏ The Fox Steals Home
❏ Hard Drive to Short
❏ The Kid Who Only
   Hit Homers
❏ Little Lefty
❏ Long Stretch at First Base
❏ Look Who's Playing
   First Base
❏ Miracle at the Plate
❏ No Arm in Left Field
❏ Shortstop from Tokyo
❏ The Submarine Pitch
❏ Too Hot to Handle
❏ The Year Mom Won
   the Pennant

Basketball

❏ The Basket Counts
❏ Johnny Long Legs
❏ Long Shot for Paul
❏ Red-Hot Hightops

Dirt Bike Racing

❏ Dirt Bike Racer
❏ Dirt Bike Runaway

Football

❏ Catch That Pass!
❏ The Counterfeit Tackle
❏ Football Fugitive
❏ The Great Quarterback
   Switch
❏ Tight End
❏ Touchdown for Tommy
❏ Tough to Tackle

Ice Hockey

❏ Face-Off
❏ The Hockey Machine
❏ Ice Magic

Soccer

❏ Soccer Halfback

Track

❏ Run, Billy, Run

All available in paperback from Little, Brown and Company

Join the Matt Christopher Fan Club!

To become an official member of the Matt Christopher Fan Club,
send a self-addressed, stamped envelope (10 x 13, 3 oz. of postage) to:

Matt Christopher Fan Club
34 Beacon Street
Boston, MA 02108